CRASH OF DEATH

"Linette," Slocum started to say.

"What's wrong, John?"

"I don't know. I thought I heard something."

Then he saw the movement at the window. Slocum pushed himself away from Linette as hard as he could. He crashed to the floor just as the window exploded in a shower of glass. He grabbed for his holstered six-shooter when the second blast from the shotgun came through the window.

"Linette!" he cried.

Sightless blue eyes stared at him.

The buckshot had caught her square in the chest.

Perkins

OTHER BOOKS BY JAKE LOGAN

JAKE LOGAN

VENGEANCE ROAD

BERKLEY BOOKS, NEW YORK

VENGEANCE ROAD

A Berkley Book / published by arrangement with
the author

PRINTING HISTORY
Berkley edition / July 1990

ISBN: 0-425-12174-7

A BERKLEY BOOK® TM 757,375
Berkley Books are published by The Berkley Publishing Group,
200 Madison Avenue, New York, New York 10016.
The name "BERKLEY" and the "B" logo
are trademarks belonging to Berkley Publishing Corporation.

PRINTED IN THE UNITED STATES OF AMERICA

10 9 8 7 6 5 4 3 2 1

1

John Slocum couldn't keep from looking in the woman's direction. He had been battered and beaten and rocked and whipped into one aching lump riding on the railroad, and she was just about the best thing he'd seen since Kansas City.

If he was any judge, the dark-haired, blue-eyed woman was doing her share of looking him over, too.

The train let out a mournful wail as it rattled up to a water stop. Slocum stood and stretched. He had been on the train for four days. The woman had been on for only the past few hours. Thoughts raced through his mind. Where was she going? Probably Denver, just as he was. From the cut of her fine dress and the intricately wrought gold brooch at her swanlike throat, she wasn't hurting for money.

Slocum touched his vest pocket. His brother's legacy, a watch, rested there along with a half dozen gold double eagles. Slocum wasn't hurting for money none, either. Still, it wouldn't do just to walk up to her, not a fine-looking, dignified woman like her. He'd bide his time and everything would fall right into his lap.

He heard the conductor calling that the steam engine had filled its tank and was ready to pull out again. Just as the pressure built and the train began its slow, grinding forward motion, the woman stood. The engineer let loose the clutch and the train lurched hard.

For an instant Slocum was speechless. The woman lost her balance and fell across him. He broke out laughing as he helped her to the seat across from him.

The woman primly tucked a few strands of her midnight-dark hair under her hat and glowered at him.

"And what do you find so funny, sir?"

"My apologies," he said, touching the brim of his black, dusty Stetson. "I was thinking something might fall into my lap. I didn't reckon it would happen so soon."

She stared at him for an instant, then the sour expression faded and brightness shone forth like the very sun. She finally broke out in a laugh, too.

"I must say I was thinking along similar lines. Are you traveling alone, sir?"

"Slocum, ma'am, John Slocum."

"My name is Linette Clayton. Please, do we need to rest on such formality after our . . . informal introduction?" Her bright blue eyes danced. Slocum decided the rest of the trip to Denver might be far more enjoyable than he had anticipated.

"Reckon not," Slocum said. He shifted seats, and Linette moved closer so that they could talk over the screech of the train's steel wheels and the pounding of the engine. More than once Linette reached over and flicked a burning cinder off him that had come through the open window. Slocum didn't mind but pulled up shy of doing the same for her. He always told her of the burning specks as they landed on her stylish dress.

Before he realized it, the train pulled into the Denver railroad station.

He helped Linette down from the train and saw to her luggage, two large trunks that were heavy enough to carry most women's entire worldly belongings.

"You moving here?" he asked as he heaved one trunk up and onto his back.

"Please, John, there's no need for you to carry them. I'll get a porter."

"No bother," he said. The trunk was heavy but not too heavy for him.

"I insist. And no, I'm only visiting Denver for a few days. My sister is getting married this coming Sunday."

"It's only Wednesday," Slocum pointed out. "How are you going to fill the time till Sunday?"

Linette's wide blue eyes twinkled. "Where are you staying?" she asked.

"Reckon I'll stay at the Palmer House. I usually do when I'm in Denver. About the best hotel the city has to offer."

"What a coincidence," Linette said. "That's where I'm staying also." She smiled even wider and said, "I reckon that solves the problem of how to while away the hours until Sunday, doesn't it? I never was one for visiting family."

"Your sister must want to see you," Slocum said.

"Angelica isn't expecting me until Saturday. I just happened to make better time than anticipated."

"Let's go find out if the Palmer House has two rooms."

"Yes, let's," Linette said. From her tone she hoped that they had only one—a large one for the pair of them.

"Please, John, don't deny me. I want to go!" Linette Clayton had a way of wheedling what she wanted from him.

"It's dangerous for a lady."

"Lady, me?" She looked positively devilish dressed in the merry widow. She spun around and let him get a good look at her trim waist, full breasts, and long, ivory legs.

Linette reached down and drew up a black silk stocking along one leg, slowly, sensuously, inviting him to come help her. Slocum lay back on the bed and just watched.

The past three days had been more than he expected. The Palmer House had dozens of free rooms; he and Linette had ended up in a suite together. For her, money was no object. He saw the roll of greenbacks she carried and knew she came from a wealthy family. Most parents would never allow an unmarried daughter to go gallivanting off unattended across the country, even to an older sister's wedding, but Linette was strong-willed and got what she wanted.

Slocum was glad they both wanted the same thing. He wouldn't want to cross her.

He watched in real appreciation as she performed her reverse striptease. Both stockings were pulled up and fastened to the garters dangling from the black merry widow. She turned her back to him and bent over, her finely rounded bottom wiggling just enough to entice him, to promise him paradise if he would only give in to her demands.

"I need to make the money. I'm not rich. Fact is, Linette, I'm almost down to my last dollar."

"I've got money. But that's not the point," she said almost primly. He had to laugh at her attitude. She was prancing around like a saloon hussy and yet she sounded like an unmarried schoolmarm, all prissy and proper.

"That is the point. I don't let a woman pay my way. It's not right."

Linette smiled wickedly. "Let me go along. I just want to see you when you're gambling."

Slocum relented, saying, "You've seen me gambling. Just being with you is a big one." And for him it was. He was finding himself becoming fonder of Linette with every passing minute. She was about everything a man could want. She was smart and pretty and her family had money.

The first two reasons mattered more to Slocum than the third, but the money didn't hurt any.

"Then I can come along? I've never seen a real poker game."

"You can come," he said, eyeing her long, stocking-clad legs and trim waist and ample breasts. Win or lose, he knew when they returned to this room he'd be a winner—and so would Linette.

Slocum heaved himself off the bed and settled into his own clothes, strapping on his cross-draw holster and settling his Colt Navy in the soft leather sheath. He went to his bag and poked through it until he found a heavy .44 derringer. This went into his vest pocket, next to his watch. He wasn't expecting trouble—but by being ready for it he might prevent the unexpected.

This of all nights, with Linette along, he didn't hanker to get into a brawl with any drunken cowpoke who thought he was being cheated.

His fine linen jacket settled on his broad shoulders. He shrugged once or twice to get it into place, then reached slowly for his six-shooter. Everything was ready. He turned to Linette and was surprised to find that she had changed from a half-dressed harlot into a fully clothed lady. He let out a long, low whistle in appreciation.

"You like this outfit? My papa sent to France for it. I've never worn it before." She batted her long, dark eyelashes at him. "I never had an occasion to."

"I'm flattered," Slocum said, "but we might be going into some rough places. The private clubs in Denver don't let just anyone in from off the street, but the riffraff still gets in." He didn't bother telling her that some of the worst places were those catering only to the upper-class gamblers.

"They'll let you in. You look as if you belong." Linette came over and adjusted Slocum's lapels and pulled a bit of nonexistent lint from his sleeve. "You look dashing. Who'd deny you entry into any club?"

Slocum snorted derisively. He hadn't been entirely frank with her about his past. The number of wanted posters floating around Colorado and the West numbered in the thousands. A small percentage of them had his likeness on them. Totaled up, he might have as much as five hundred dollars reward on his head. Some of the rewards were justified; his life hadn't been lily-white. Some were trumped-up charges, or warrants for men Slocum had ridden with. He found himself with outlaws more often than lawmen—and truth to tell, he preferred it that way.

Slocum offered Linette his arm and they left the Palmer House, walking the twilight streets of Denver. Slocum had no particular destination in mind, but he had an instinct about finding the poker games with the richest stakes—and ones where the players didn't know the odds as well as he did. He and Linette had dinner at a fashionable café a few blocks from the Palmer House, then wandered in the direction of Larimer Square, the true center of town.

"It looks different," Linette said softly. "It's so exciting—and so deliciously dangerous."

"Sinful, too," Slocum added, hearing more in what the beautiful woman was saying than just her words. She had never been allowed to experience the thrill of living at the edge, of living by her wits and not knowing if she would survive. Slocum realized he gave her a small measure of this, at least vicariously.

And what did she give him? Slocum forced his thoughts away from that. He was becoming too attached to Linette Clayton. He had known her for only a short while, and yet it seemed as if they had been soul mates all their lives.

"Here," he said suddenly. He stopped and pointed down a dark alley. "There's a big game down this way. If you want, you can go back to the Palmer House."

"No!"

"All right, but don't say anything to anyone. This isn't the finest section of town, and the men tend to be on the rough-and-tumble side." He didn't add that the women were likely all whores, too.

Slocum and Linette made their way down the litter-strewn alley. A heavy iron-plated door with a single peephole in it was the only sign that people came and went. Slocum knocked. The peephole turned into a small circle of dim yellow light, then darkened quickly as someone pushed his eye to the hole.

"I'm looking for a game." Slocum opened his jacket and slid his wallet out partially. The wallet dropped back but a greenback remained in plain view. The bars inside the door grated and the massive door swung open on well-oiled hinges.

"What—"

Slocum squeezed down on Linette's arm to silence her. A meaty hand reached out and snatched away the scrip. Only then did the door open wide to admit them.

Slocum guided Linette past the bouncer, a hulking man with a beetle brow. He carried a heavy club at his waist and had a sawed-off shotgun slung on a leather strap over his left shoulder. Linette shivered as she saw how heavily armed the man was. Slocum pulled her along the dimly lit corridor, and then they entered a lavishly decorated parlor, bright and cheerful and filled with people intent on losing their money.

"Good evening, sir," said a well-dressed man Slocum took to be the manager. He doubted the owner of this gambling den would be present unless something special was happening.

"Evening. I'm looking for a little action. Faro, perhaps, or even a game of stud poker."

"You're in luck, sir. This way, please." The manager

motioned for them to precede him. Slocum knew the man's eyes were on the lovely Linette. Slocum didn't mind. It gave him a chance to study the layout, as if it were a bank and he was going to rob it. He had no such intentions, but the preparations the owner had made to keep his money told Slocum much about the amount of money that flowed across these gaming tables.

If he was any judge, many thousands of dollars a night changed hands here.

Linette stood behind him, flushed and excited at the prospect of seeing a side of life she had never experienced. By the end of the evening, Slocum was three hundred dollars to the good. He pushed back and stood, sweeping up his earnings and stuffing them into his side coat pocket.

"Where you going?" demanded the big loser in the game, a florid man who bet badly and telegraphed every good hand he was dealt by squinting and muscle twitches.

Slocum pressed close to Linette and whispered, "Take the derringer from my vest pocket. Don't use it unless you have to." She slipped it out of his brocade waistcoat with a trembling hand and hit it under her flowing skirt. Only then did Slocum turn to face the angry man across the table.

"It's well nigh dawn. I'm going to bed. I'd advise you to do the same. You look tuckered out."

"Sit down. We're going to play until I win my money back."

"That'd be a cold day in hell, friend," Slocum said, his words colder than the eventuality he mentioned.

The ruddy-faced man rose, kicking his chair back. Slocum heard Linette gasp at the challenge. He moved to the side so she wasn't in the line of fire. His coat opened to reveal the ebony-handled Colt Navy hanging at his hip.

"I don't want any trouble, but I won't have you telling me what to do," Slocum said.

"I want to win back my money. I *need* it!"

"Then you've learned a valuable lesson tonight. Don't bet money you can't afford to lose. Now, what's it going to be?" Slocum straightened his shoulders and pulled back his coat so his six-shooter hung free.

The man licked his lips. His hand trembled above his own pistol.

Silence fell on the room. And then came a loud cocking sound that echoed louder than any gunshot. All eyes turned to Linette. She held the derringer in both hands, the gun pointed directly at the man facing Slocum.

"It's all right, Linette," Slocum said. "Our friend has had too much to drink, and he's dog-tired. He was just leaving."

"You . . . you and the bitch robbed me of my money. I won't forget this!" The man backed away, then spun and ran off. A door slammed a few seconds later. Only then did Slocum relax. He went to Linette and took the derringer from her shaking fingers.

"You didn't have to do that," Slocum said. "He was just sucking wind at both ends. He didn't mean anything by it."

"I could have killed him," Linette said, eyes feverish. "It was frightening."

"It was also exciting, wasn't it?" Slocum said softly.

She turned her face up to his and whispered. "Yes!"

Slocum wasn't sure who was in the bigger hurry to get back to their hotel room. He had barely opened the door when Linette pushed past him, working frantically to get her dress open. In the dim light coming through the dawn-lit window, Slocum saw Linette step out of the dress. Again she was dressed only in the corset and stockings. He felt himself responding at the sight of so much woman. He closed the door.

He got no farther. Linette was all over him. Her lips

sought his, even as her hands worked to get his gun belt free. Her haste to undo his trousers was almost comical.

"Whoa," Slocum said, pulling free. "We've got all night."

"I want you *now*," she whispered in a husky voice. She dropped to her knees and began wrestling off his pants. He slipped free of his jacket about the same time Linette blew hotly across his groin. Then her mouth engulfed him.

Slocum staggered slightly. She hung on, following him on her knees. Her hands circled his legs, then gripped his muscular buttocks, pulling him forward. The lava-hot feelings building inside him told Slocum he'd lose control quickly if the woman didn't slow down.

He laced his fingers through her dark hair and slackened the pace. Her head bobbed up and down with more deliberation, but her tongue worked on his most sensitive flesh until he felt like a stick of dynamite about ready to explode.

"I want you, John. This is the most stimulating night of my life. *I want you!*"

She worked her way up his body, kissing and licking and lightly nibbling at his flesh until she again stood. Her fleshy breasts crushed against his broad chest. Her lips locked on his in a passionate kiss that sent Slocum's heart pounding even faster.

He reached down and found her stocking-clad legs. With an easy heave he got Linette off her feet and into his arms. He carried her to the wide bed and put her down lightly. Sinking beside her, he began worrying at the silken ties on her corset.

"Don't bother," she said. "I want you *here*, John. Now. With *this*." She took his hand and placed it on the dark-furred triangle between her legs. Then she gripped his throbbing shaft and squeezed hard. Slocum gasped in reaction when she began pulling him insistently toward her.

He didn't want to resist, but he did want to make the

sensations racing up and down his body last a mite longer. Linette was too insistent. The brief skirmish after the poker game had made her hot, and she wasn't to be denied.

Her legs drifted apart and she kept pulling him toward her. Slocum slipped between the soft thighs, then gasped when she locked her heels behind his back. She pulled him inward with surprising power.

"I don't want you to stop, not ever, John. I want you always!"

Slocum moved his hips up a little and felt his manhood brush the damp fur he had touched earlier. Linette rocked back on the bed, lifting up her rounded buttocks to make entry easier. Slocum shoved forward harder than he usually did. He wanted to dampen her fervor just a bit, to give him time to catch his breath.

The roughness delighted Linette even more. She was panting with desire. A hot flush had risen to her breasts and shoulders. Her eyes were tightly screwed shut and she was moaning passionately. The way her soft inner flesh crushed down on him told Slocum there wasn't going to be any lengthy lovemaking.

Linette wanted it, and fast.

He gave it to her. His hips levered back and forth, driving him deep into her humid interior. Every hard thrust brought a new exclamation of rapture to Linette's lips. She raked his back with her fingernails. She hunched up to meet him and rolled her hips to drive him even deeper into her.

Slocum fell into a steady rhythm that set fire to his meaty shaft. The friction, along with the pressure from the female flesh surrounding him, tore at his control. White-hot fluids churned in his balls. He tried to hold back but couldn't. Linette had done too much to arouse him.

He spilled his seed into her yearning core just as Linette shrieked out her own joy. She clung to him for several seconds, then relaxed. She lay back on the bed, her eyes even brighter than they had been before.

"That was unbelievable, John. Let's do it again."

"In a minute," he said, trying to catch his breath.

Linette curled up close to him, her slender fingers stroking over him and bringing new sensations to his body that he had never felt before. She worked her wonders and got him erect again in record time.

"You are coming with me to my sister's wedding this afternoon?" she asked.

The question was so unexpected, Slocum couldn't find words to answer.

"Good, I'm glad that's settled," she said. He started to speak, but she cut off the protest in the most delightful way possible.

They made love twice more before the sun shone brightly through the window, bathing them in soft spring Colorado sunlight.

2

"Get up, John," urged Linette Clayton. "There's not much time to get ready."

Slocum rolled over in the wide bed and stared at her. Linette washed her face and hands. Other than the droplets of water dancing on her face and in the dark bangs slipping down over her forehead, she was deliciously naked. Slocum felt himself beginning to respond to the tempting sight.

"Come back to bed," he said. "There's no place we have to be."

"There is too," she said sternly. She toweled off and went to the tall cedar-lined wardrobe in one corner of the room. She shuffled through the dresses hanging there and took out an elegant blue silk and brocade dress Slocum hadn't seen before. Tiny wisps of memory came back to him. He groaned.

"I don't want to go to any wedding," he said, remembering that Linette's sister was getting married that afternoon. He reached over and found his vest. Fumbling the watch out from the pocket, he saw that it was almost noon.

Angelica Clayton's wedding was supposed to start at two o'clock sharp.

"You promised."

"I didn't," he said. "Not exactly."

"Very well," Linette said, not turning to look at him. She continued dressing, as if he had made a small comment about the weather and nothing more. The idea that she didn't argue began to gnaw at his guts. If she had put up any fight, he would have felt justified in going back on his word.

Even though she had wormed the promise out of him while he was out of his pants, he had promised. Slocum wasn't the kind of man to renege lightly on a pledge he had given, but he didn't want to go to any wedding. He was uneasy with the notion of having Linette beside him. Weddings did strange things to women. The ones who weren't married got to thinking about it. And the ones who were, got to looking around at the unmarried men, sizing them up, wondering what they'd missed being married to their husbands.

Either condition spelled trouble.

"Linette?"

"I'm in a hurry, John. Just go on back to sleep, if that's what you want to do. I'm sure last night tired you out."

"That it did," he said, heaving his feet off the bed. "But I promised I'd go."

"There's no need. If you want to stay here, do so."

Slocum grumbled and complained as he got up and found his fancy britches. They ought to be good enough for a wedding. He began dressing, not quite swearing out loud the whole while. He turned once and caught sight of Linette's face in a mirror. A wide smile had crept across it. The bitch was enjoying tormenting him like this!

What bothered Slocum more than the idea of having to go to a wedding was beginning to think what it would be like getting hitched to Linette. She was one fine, handsome woman, and she'd made her feelings for him quite clear. She was a rich girl set free on her own for the first time. This had made her a bit wild and reckless. But Slocum enjoyed her company. The few days they'd spent together were better than any other time he could remember, not that there were many happy memories.

He sighed deeply. Back home in Calhoun, Georgia, had been about the best of times for him. He had enjoyed working the land on the family farm. His brother, Robert, was about the best hunter in four counties, and he rivaled their father in being able to get crops almost to jump up out of the ground.

That had been before the war. Afterward had been a different matter. His brother had died at Little Round Top, the victim of Pickett's stupidity. Slocum had ridden with Quantrill's Raiders until they gut-shot him for protesting the Lawrenceville, Kansas, raid where women and children had been cut down mercilessly. Recovering had taken time.

By the time he'd gotten back to Calhoun County, his parents were dead—but working the farm wasn't in the cards.

Slocum forced himself to think of more cheerful things than the carpetbagger judge trying to take the farm because of "unpaid taxes." The judge and his hired gunman had been left buried on the ridge by the springhouse, and Slocum had ridden west, never looking back.

Since then he had been a fugitive from the law and seldom had time to do more than look back over his shoulder to see what bounty hunter was catching up with him.

Linette Clayton made him think of other things, better things. For the first time since the end of the war, he considered settling down. He could do a lot worse than someone like her.

"I'm ready. Are you sure you want to go, John?"

"I'm sure." He settled his cross-draw holster and the

pistol in it, then checked for the derringer in his vest pocket. He wasn't expecting trouble at the wedding, but getting to the church might be a bit touchy. The rubicund man from the night before had had blood in his eye. Slocum had seen his share of drunks in card games. The loser in the poker game hadn't been all that intoxicated. He was just mean and one damned poor loser.

"You look very fashionable," she said, eyeing him critically. He thought she didn't want to show up with a man who had even a hair out of place.

He kissed her. She responded just enough to let him know she appreciated him keeping his word, then pushed back. "Let's hurry. I don't want to be late."

"We've got time," he said, looking at his watch again. It was hardly one o'clock.

"You forget. My sister expected me yesterday. She'll be worried that I wasn't able to make her wedding."

"The happiest day of her life ought to be shared with family," Slocum allowed.

"I want Angelica to meet you, too," Linette said, squeezing down on his arm. Slocum experienced the mixed feelings again. He knew what Linette meant. She wanted to show off her catch.

"What's the man your sister is marrying like?"

"I know very little about Mr. Norton, save that he is an executive officer of a mining company."

Slocum nodded. That meant Linette's older sister had done well for herself. There weren't too many mines set up with directors and officers that weren't turning a substantial profit. The usual agreement had the officers sharing in the mine's profits, which made many of them wealthy men without ever having to enter the death pits where the gold and silver came from.

"Do we have time for a bite to eat?" Slocum asked. "It's been a spell since we did."

"Too much exercise?" she said chidingly.

"I know, I know, you're anxious to see your sister."
Slocum relented and escorted her downstairs. He reached
into the right pocket of his jacket and found the roll of
greenbacks he had won the night before. He peeled off a
single note and gave it to the bell captain, to find them a
proper carriage. In a few minutes they were clattering
through the streets of Denver on their way to the First
Presbyterian Church.

Slocum tried to relax but couldn't. Linette grew increas-
ingly restive, anxious to see her sister. She almost shot from
the carriage when it pulled up in front of the whitewashed
clapboard church. Slocum paid the driver and hurried after
her.

Linette burst into the vestibule and accosted the first person she found. Without even speaking to Slocum, she rushed
off to a small room at the side of the church.

"That must be Linette," a man sitting by the door said.
"Angelica has been going crazy with worry over her."

"I reckon her sister is the only family able to attend the
wedding."

"Reckon so," the man said, leaning back in his chair,
precariously balancing on the back two legs. "Their father
isn't well, and their mother refused to come out here and
leave him alone."

Slocum studied the man more closely. He knew a great
deal more about the Clayton family misfortune than Slocum
did.

"Excuse me. I'm being rude." The man rocked forward
and came to his feet. "The name's Ingram, Ben Ingram.
I'm the best man."

"John Slocum. I'm . . . with Linette," he finished
lamely. He wasn't sure exactly what his status was with the
pretty woman.

"Glad to meet you. You in mining?"

"No," Slocum said, cautious. "I understand Angelica's groom is, though. Do you work with him?"

"That I do. Rupert's first vice-president of the Iron-Silver Mining Company, and I'm operations manager."

"I'm not familiar with the Iron-Silver Company," said Slocum, wanting to keep the subject away from himself. Something about Ingram's attitude put Slocum on edge.

"We own several mines over Leadville way," he said. "We're taking more than a quarter of a million dollars a month in silver from just one of our mines. At this rate we'll need even more staff here in Denver."

"It certainly sounds as if you're doing well—and that Angelica is a lucky woman."

"It's Rupe who's the lucky one," said Ingram. "I don't know how a galoot like him rates a woman like her."

Before Slocum could reply, he heard the rattle of a carriage outside the church. He glanced through the double doors and saw a nervous man hurrying up. The carriage driver lounged around under a spreading elm tree, making Slocum think that this would be the way the newlyweds would leave the church.

And the well-dressed, nervous man approaching had to be Rupert Norton.

"Rupe, good news," called out Ingram. "Angelica's sister got here a few minutes ago."

"I'm glad. I'd never have heard the end of it if Angelica had to use my sister as maid of honor."

Slocum watched the two men huddle together, groom and best man, and formed a picture of them he didn't much like. They were polite but distant. He had seen their ilk before. They were soft men, knowing nothing of the miners' plight in the filthy, dangerous mines. All they did was take the metal earned by the sweat and blood of others and invest it in who knows what other ventures.

Money making money. Slocum wasn't adverse to that,

but men like Norton and Ingram showed none of the compassion toward anyone who wasn't of their social strata.

He knew he might be making an unfair estimate of the men's character. Angelica, if she was anything like her sister, would be an exceptional woman. She wouldn't want a callous, uncaring man as husband. Slocum decided he'd hold off on his final decision about Norton until he got to know him better.

"I wish everyone'd get here," Norton said, rubbing his hands together. "This is worse than waiting for the first assay from the Little King."

Ingram laughed harshly. "Yeah, sure, all that meant was whether we were bankrupt or rich."

"You know what I mean," snapped Norton.

Slocum heard nothing of good-humored joking in the men's tones. They seemed put out that they had to take time from their money-making to go through with the wedding.

The guests began arriving. Slocum watched the well-heeled crowd and felt out of place. There wasn't a man or woman in the church who hadn't paid more for their clothing than he had won the night before. Jewelry on both the men and women was lavish. The men wore diamond stickpins and cufflinks made from nuggets of raw gold. It didn't take much to guess that they were all involved in the mining industry, just like Rupert Norton and his best man.

The women ran the gamut from homely to pretty, but none held a candle to Linette. Slocum knew he might be a bit prejudiced on the subject, but not by much.

The wedding guests seated themselves. An expectant hush fell over the church. Slocum slipped in and found a seat at the side of the church. He could see the altar where Norton and Ingram stood. Rupert Norton looked the world like he wanted to be somewhere else. Slocum put this to wedding-day jitters.

The organ started playing and Linette came in. She flashed

Slocum a bright smile. He thought she looked so damned beautiful, his heart almost leapt from his chest. Behind her came her sister, on the arm of an older man standing in for their father.

Angelica Clayton bore a strong resemblance to her sister. Slocum studied her critically. She was older, but not by much. Her dark hair wasn't quite as lustrous and her cheeks were a bit too high for Slocum's taste, but there was no denying their relationship. They were as alike as peas in a pod.

Angelica got to the front of the church. Slocum didn't pay a lot of attention to the ceremony. His eyes were on Linette. And from time to time she looked back in his direction, her gaze bold and provocative. Slocum wasn't quite sure what was on his mind, but it was obvious what thoughts raced through Linette's. She had found a prospective husband in John Slocum, and she'd elbow any of the other single women out of the way to catch her sister's bouquet.

The minister was just about ready to pronounce Angelica the wife of Rupert Norton when the outer doors of the church slammed open loudly. Slocum heaved himself off the hard wood pew to go shut the doors. A gust of wind must have blown them open.

He was aware of heads turning toward him as he made his way out.

Then all hell broke loose.

Loud whoops were followed by the roar of shotguns. Slocum reacted rather than thought. His hand flashed to his six-shooter and drew it as he dived down behind the last row of pews.

"Don't nobody go doin' anything dumb," roared one roughly dressed man who was wearing a dirty blue bandanna over his face. "We're here to do a little robbin', nothing more."

Two others followed him into the church, their scatter-guns leveled. Slocum held his fire. He could cut down one of the men, but the other two owl hoots would open up on the wedding guests before he could get off a second shot.

He rolled under the pew and wiggled forward. The men had cast a quick look down the aisle when they came in and hadn't seen him. He was behind them. Now he had to make that element of surprise count.

"Fork over them jewels, ma'am" came the brusque command from the leader. Slocum chanced a quick look over the top of the pew and saw Linette with her arms around Angelica. He frowned. This didn't seem the way it ought to be.

At first he couldn't figure out what should have been happening, then he saw Norton and Ingram. Their faces had blanched whiter than any sheet, and they were edging along the altar toward the back of the church. They were turning tail and running, leaving the women to face the shotgun-toting robbers.

Slocum seethed when he saw such cowardice. He drew the derringer from his vest pocket and dropped flat on his belly and began working his way toward the front of the church along the outer aisle, making certain the robbers didn't see him.

Before he reached the front, one robber yelled, "Don't try it, you son of a bitch!"

Shotguns roared and the church filled with the smoke from their discharge. From the mechanical clicking and shell ejection, Slocum knew the three men worked well together. One fired while another reloaded and the third watched, protecting the other two. This wasn't any normal robbery.

Angelica shrieked and rushed forward. Slocum caught sight of Linette out of the corner of his eye and knew she was following her sister. He couldn't wait any longer. He blasted to his feet and leveled both the .44 derringer and his trusty Colt Navy.

Lead spat from the derringer's barrel and caught one robber high in the shoulder. The impact of the heavy slug sent the man spinning around. Slocum tried to finish him off with the more accurate Colt but knew he'd missed the instant he pulled the trigger.

The roar from the blazing shotguns deafened him. The guests all stood and blocked his line of fire. He jumped onto a seat and tried to get a clean shot at the robbers.

In a flash he saw what was happening. Both Norton and Ingram were down. Angelica knelt beside her groom as he struggled weakly to get to his feet. Two shotguns swung around and centered on the unlucky couple.

They fired before Slocum could. He saw Norton and Angelica die in a shower of blood as the heavy buckshot ripped into them.

Then the world turned to awful pain and blackness as he felt 00 buck strike him in the side. He tried to fire, but his fingers had turned nerveless. He toppled backward, as stiff as any tree cut down by a lumberjack.

The church faded from sight and the howls of anger and pain receded. Slocum passed out.

3

All Slocum knew was red-hot pain cutting into his side. He tried to thrash around and force it away. Steel bands fastened on his brawny wrists and held him down easily. The more he fought, the weaker he got. Through the haze of searing pain came faint noises. He concentrated on them and finally made sense out of the words.

"Stop fighting me, damn your eyes. This is for your own good."

The words carried more torment with them. Slocum shuddered and let the pain wash over him, like waves against the shoreline. Accepting that he could do nothing, he struggled to open his eyes. Light burned and threatened to make his head explode.

"You're coming around. Good. You took quite a load of buckshot from those yahoos. Didn't know if you'd make it or not. The wounds were nasty ones, even if there weren't any bones busted. Should have guessed you wouldn't up and die on me. You're a tough hombre."

"Who . . . ?" Slocum tried to sit up and instantly regretted it. The pain had been bad before. Now it almost overwhelmed him, sending him back to oblivion. He quieted, working on what had to be done next.

Eyes. Slocum opened them and looked around. He was in a doctor's surgery. A skeleton hung on a hook near the door. Cabinets loaded with instruments and medicines lined the walls. And nearby, on the table where Slocum lay, were bloodied towels and steel surgical tools. The doctor had been working on a patient.

Slocum wasn't far enough gone to wonder who. From the throbbing in his side, he knew who had been cut.

"Want a pull on this?" A man came into Slocum's field of vision. A bottle of Billy Thompson's Whiskey floated in front of him. Slocum reached out for it and missed. "I'll help you. It's potent firewater. Take only a sip at first."

The fiery lance stabbing into Slocum's guts did more to revive him than anything else.

"What happened?"

"That's a question the law is going to be asking you." The doctor took a quick sip of the whiskey, then held the bottle out to Slocum again, who almost choked as the liquor flooded down his throat.

"Three men. They came in to rob everyone in the wedding party. For some reason they started shooting and killing people." Even as Slocum spoke, he knew that he had the answer to why the three bandits had turned violent. The answer just drifted away, elusive as any butterfly when he tried to put it into words.

"Don't much care about that. Getting you into shape is my job. The federal marshal will want you to go over all that. You were one of the lucky ones, believe it or not."

"Others died?"

"Four others. Damn shame to ruin a fine wedding like that. Want another slug of whiskey?"

Slocum did. And then the lights began to dim, and he

slid over the edge of darkness once more, this time to sleep deeply.

He sat up in the straight-backed chair and tried not to let the pain distract him. He wasn't too successful.

"So, Mr. Slocum, you tried to stop them. Ever think you might have caused them to shoot up the church like they did?" The federal marshal was a dour man, powerfully built and with heavy eyebrows that looked like wiggling caterpillars when he frowned. And he was frowning more than Slocum cared for.

"It didn't seem that way to me. They missed me when they came in. When a man starts waving a shotgun around, you've got to believe he intends to use it."

"So you're claiming to be a fucking hero, is that it?" The marshal grunted harshly and shook his head. Lank brown hair flopped as he denied that Slocum was any kind of hero for what he'd done. "I'll tell you what I think. I think you riled them, and *that's* why they opened up on the wedding party."

"Did they get much in the way of loot?"

"A few trinkets. You spooked them good."

Slocum controlled his anger. One good thing had come of this interview. His rage burned away the pain and allowed him to concentrate.

"Who died? The doctor wouldn't say anything more than four people died." Slocum was afraid of the answer. He had been in the doctor's office all evening, and Linette hadn't come to see him. He had to fear the worst and prepare himself for the marshal telling of the lovely woman's murder.

The notion that Linette had died in the gunfire wore heavily on him. What if the marshal was right? What if he had caused the shooting? He might have been responsible for the death of the woman he was coming to love—and who loved him.

"The groom got it first. A man name of Rupert Norton. He was a big shot with a mining company. His best man got cut down, too."

"Ingram," Slocum said. "I met him just before the wedding started."

"Ingram," acknowledged the marshal. "Then there was a man in the pews by the name of Frederickson. He worked for the same mining company as a bookkeeper."

"There was one more. Who was it?" demanded Slocum, prepared to hear the worst.

"The bride. Angelica Clayton was her name. Hell of a way to spend your wedding day, getting blowed apart by a scattergun."

"What of her sister, Linette?"

The marshal sent his eyebrows crawling up and down as he scowled and studied the sheet of paper in front of him. "Her sister was maid of honor. She wasn't even hurt."

Slocum experienced a rush of contradictory emotions. He was glad Linette had escaped unharmed, but he was also bewildered that she hadn't come to call on him. He had asked the doctor in a roundabout way if there'd been any visitors while he was unconscious. The bushy-browed marshal had been the only one wanting to see him.

"I've told you all I can. The doctor says I ought to rest. I lost a fair amount of blood."

"Reckon so," the marshal allowed. "There's not going to be too much I can do unless somebody gets drunk and shoots off his mouth."

"I can go?"

"You can go to hell for all I care." The marshal glared at him. Slocum rose stiffly and left, aware that the lawman considered him the cause of the four deaths. Slocum ran the events over and over in his head as he slowly walked back to the Palmer House. He couldn't see it that way. More might have died if he hadn't shot at the leader.

Slocum saw the scene perfectly. He had done more than wing the second man. He had sent at least two bullets into his chest. The robber was more than hurting—he might have died.

Slocum took cold comfort from this. If he had been able, he would have killed all three. He was sorry now that he hadn't followed his instinct and slipped into the aisle behind them and backshot the sons of bitches. It wouldn't have been honorable, but it would have saved four innocent human beings from dying.

He didn't want to draw any attention to himself, so he entered the hotel through a side entrance and slipped up the back stairs. For the first time he was sorry his room was on the fourth floor. The effort of climbing the stairs robbed him of the strength he had hoarded. Slocum was panting and weak by the time he turned the knob on the door.

Entering, he half expected to see Linette Clayton waiting for him. He was disappointed. She was nowhere to be seen—and her clothing hadn't been touched.

"She's got to come back for it," he said to himself. He got out of his ragged, blood-soaked clothing and threw it in the corner. He wouldn't be wearing it again. He found sturdier trail clothing and donned it. The cotton shirt felt soft and cool next to his skin, and the rough canvas britches reminded him of times on the trail, living under the stars, away from the so-called civilization that saw men with shotguns murdering members of wedding parties.

He slung his gun belt around his waist and reached across to see if he could pull out the Colt in the holster. Stabs of hurt shot into his chest. The buckshot had run along his ribs but hadn't done more than chew up his skin. He'd lost a fair amount of blood, but eating a good steak would do much to restore his stamina.

Slocum looked again at Linette's belongings, then left the room. He had questions to ask.

He wandered the streets, ignoring the fancier section of Denver and moving toward the north end of Larimer Square, where workingmen might gather for a drink. He found the Stolen Nugget Saloon and looked inside. From the way the men were dressed, Slocum guessed they were miners.

Three of the four who had been killed worked for the Iron-Silver Mining Company. This might be a good place to find out more about the company and its officers.

The stench of spilled beer and stale vomit rose to his nostrils as he pushed his way deeper into the saloon. He found an empty table and collapsed into the chair. The rickety chair almost gave way under him. He didn't care. He was still weak from the shooting.

"Howdy, mister, new in town?" The saloon whore was too skinny for his tastes. The heat in her eyes told Slocum she had habits he probably wouldn't care for but that he could exploit.

"Not too lonely, but I could do with a spell of talking," he said, pointing to another chair. "Let me buy you a drink."

"That's right hospitable of you." She motioned to the barkeep, who fixed Slocum a potent drink and the whore a watered-down one. Slocum didn't care. He wasn't going to be lured back into the cribs. He wanted information.

He glanced around, trying to size up the crowd. Most of the men looked to be down-on-their-luck miners. A few others might just be passing through, like him, and had stopped in for a quick drink and an even quicker roll in the hay.

The whore put down the drinks on the table. Her skin was parched and dry and it looked as if her eyes burned. Slocum guessed she had a laudanum habit. A drink might ease the inner pain, but it wouldn't do enough to her liking.

"I'm not interested," Slocum said when her hand crept under the table and up his leg toward his crotch. He grabbed her wrist and held it when she tried to pull back. "Not in that. But I might be interested in more conversation."

"You're not the law," the woman said. "I can smell 'em a mile off."

"Who do those men work for?" He motioned toward the bar.

She shrugged. "Any of a dozen companies. Most are in town to spend the money they made up in Leadville or Cripple Creek. When they're broke, they drift back to the mines."

"Seems a long ways to come just to just to belly up a bar. Is the Stolen Nugget that good a place?"

"It's got me," she said immodestly.

"And you've got a bit of this," Slocum said, sliding a pair of greenbacks across the table, "if you tell me what I want to know."

"Mister, there's not enough money to make me go against any of them." She tried to leave again, but Slocum grabbed her arm and held her firmly.

"Who do you think I am?"

"You got to work for the mining company. Why else ask about the likes of them?" She tipped her head toward the miners at the bar.

"Maybe I'm just curious. Maybe I want a job working for the Iron-Silver Mining Company."

She jerked free, rage etched on her face. "I *knew* it! You're working for the company. Get the hell out of here or I'll tell them you're here spyin' on 'em."

"I'm not. And why would I spy on them? They're just drinking."

"They're talking union business. You're not foolin' me, mister. You want to bust the union, you and all the bastards in the Iron-Silver Mining Company."

"Think they'd want to gun down the officers of the company?"

"You heard about that?"

"Four people were killed this afternoon," Slocum said, teasing the information out of her. He pulled out a ten-dollar bill and laid it on the table. She licked her dry lips, caught between loyalty to the miners' union and greed.

"The men what did the shootin' came in from Leadville special for it. They wanted the thieving bastards dead, and that's what they got. They deserved it!" she said.

"The men who were killed? Why?"

"They're trying to starve the miners with piss-poor wages. Their mines are pulling out millions of dollars in silver, and all the miners get paid is four dollars for a twelve-hour shift. That's not enough to die for."

"Not good wages," Slocum allowed, "but they can always just walk out. The mine owners would have to pony up more money or they couldn't get any silver from their mines."

"That's easy to say if you're not ass-deep in bills. The company *owns* the miners."

Slocum nodded. He had seen this in countless other places, but seldom did the miners get so aroused that they sent murderers to gun down the owners. Even the worst hothead cooled off after a trip of a hundred miles through Mosquito Pass and across the Rockies.

"So the murders of Norton, Ingram, and the other fellow—"

"Frederickson," the woman supplied.

"And Frederickson," Slocum continued, "were just the result of a labor dispute?"

"That's what everyone's saying. None of the miners like working for the company, but where else can they go? The damn mine owners hang together." She snorted, then wiped her nose on her tattered sleeve. "If you ask me, they just ought to hang."

"I can agree on part of that," Slocum said. "You know that a woman was also killed—and that it was her wedding."

"She was marryin' one of the bastards. She got what she de—" The whore clamped her mouth shut when she saw the thunderous, dark rage building on Slocum's face. She backed off, the money he had given her clutched in a bony hand.

Slocum didn't bother with the drink on the table. He levered himself to his feet and walked out slowly, aware of the hush falling over the Stolen Nugget Saloon. The whore had already told the others he was a company union-buster come to spy on them.

Slocum hoped to get out of the saloon before anyone challenged him. A heavy hand landed on his shoulder, almost knocking him to the ground. Slocum was weaker than a day-old kitten and couldn't hope to fight off a hard rock miner.

He swung to face the man. His hand had already slipped the Colt Navy from its soft leather holster. Slocum jammed the barrel hard into the man's ample gut.

"You want something from me?" Slocum asked, his eyes frozen chips of emerald.

The miner took his hand off Slocum's shoulder and backed off. "No, nothing, mister. Nothing."

Slocum had no stomach for fighting the men. If anything, his sympathy lay with them in their dispute. But he didn't cotton to murdering a man at his wedding—and killing his bride too.

He was getting light-headed and knew he ought to get back to the Palmer House and catch some sleep. It had been a hell of a day, and he wasn't up to doing more than passing out.

Slocum made his way up the stairs at the hotel. They seemed even steeper than they had before. Once more a moment's expectation rushed to give him strength as he hoped to find Linette waiting for him. And again the room was empty.

Sinking into a chair and staring out the window at the bustle of a thriving boomtown, Slocum wondered what to do. He and Linette had lost themselves in each other. He wasn't going to just give up and forget her. He wasn't sure he could.

And he sure as hell wouldn't, not after the murders at the wedding. He took it personally that the killers had shot up the church like that.

Beyond this affront, he felt he owed Linette something. Her sister and prospective brother-in-law had died. If he could do anything to right this wrong, he should. As he thought about it a slow smile came to his lips. It wouldn't be just for her, he knew. It also would be for himself.

He stretched and started to get undressed. Lying in the bed without Linette beside him would be strange. He'd gotten used to her warmth in the night.

"What the hell happened to her?" he asked out loud.

A knock came at the door, startling him. He spun, hand flashing to his six-shooter. He calmed down when the knock came again. If it had been someone looking to shoot him down, they'd just have kicked in the door.

"Who's there?" he called.

"Bellman, Mr. Slocum. There's a message for you."

Slocum opened the door, hand still holding his pistol. The uniformed bellman stood in the hall. He thrust out a yellow slip of paper.

"Thanks," Slocum said, fumbling to find a nickel. He flipped it to the bellman and closed the door. He opened the sheet of paper and saw Linette's careful handwriting marching across the page.

"Dearest John," the letter began. "Excuse me for not seeing you. I understand that you are doing well. I felt it more important to find the men who murdered Angelica. I have taken the few clothes that I thought I'd need. Please see to the rest of my belongings."

Slocum began to shake. He sat down and tried to control his renewed anger. Why had she decided to take the law into her own hands? The marshal was no great shakes as a lawman, but he had deputies to investigate for him.

More than this, why hadn't Linette trusted him to help her?

Slocum finished reading the last paragraph in the letter.

"So, dearest John, I will find those responsible and bring them to justice. When I have finished, I will meet you in Denver . . . if you've chosen to wait for me. With all my love."

Linette's name sprawled across the bottom of the letter.

Slocum crumpled the yellow sheet and tossed it into the corner of the room.

4

Slocum slept around the clock and came awake at sunset the day following the massacre at Angelica Clayton's wedding. He stretched and immediately regretted it. His ribs burned as if some Sioux warrior had shot a flaming arrow into them. He groaned when he peeled back the dressing on the wound. Four deep furrows were caked with dried blood. He staggered across the room and slopped cold water into the decorated white porcelain basin.

As carefully as he could, he soaked off the dried blood and washed the wounds. Each looked like a bear-claw scratch and hurt a thousand times worse. Slocum fought down the rising tide of torture as he worked on them, then realized he had to do more. He was on the verge of blacking out. He rummaged through his luggage and found a small silver pocket flask, still sloshing with rye whiskey. Slocum debated drinking it or using it to clean his wound.

He almost cried out when he dabbed the potent liquor on his injuries. He sat down hard and shook for a moment, then felt worlds better. The weakness passed, and he knew he was going to survive. What liquor was left in the flask was quickly finished off, burning at his throat and giving much needed strength.

Then he glanced across the room at the wardrobe door, standing half open. What remained of Linette's clothing hung inside. Slocum rose and went to the tall cedar-lined cabinet and began poking through the expensive dresses.

He wasn't sure what she had taken while he was gone. Linette had managed to pack more clothing into the two large trunks than he'd thought existed west of the Mississippi. She might have taken several outfits and he'd never know. He had always appreciated what she wore, but his interest lay more in the woman than with her store-bought finery.

Slocum's belly grumbled. He realized it had been a spell since he'd had a decent meal. He dressed gingerly, avoiding his wounded side the best he could, and then went downstairs to the Palmer House's restaurant. A thick, rare steak with all the fixings went down good. As he was leaning back to work on digesting the meal, he saw the marshal come through the beveled glass doors.

The bowlegged man looked as if he were rolling as he walked. Slocum heaved a deep sigh and reached under the table to be sure his Colt rested easy in the cross-draw holster. There wasn't any reason for the lawman to look him up—except possibly if he had found an old wanted poster shoved into some dusty file cabinet.

"Slocum," the marshal said without preamble. He sat down without waiting for an invitation. He sniffed cautiously at the remains of Slocum's meal. "You surely do eat good. Can't afford steak like that on *my* salary."

"What do you want, Marshal?"

"The doc said you were up and about. Took me this long to track you down."

"I was up in my room. Asleep," Slocum added, even

though he knew he didn't have to tell this man squat if he didn't want to.

"That's not quite the way I heard it." The marshal's eyebrows worked up and down in fuzzy ripples. "You were over at the Stolen Nugget the evening of the shooting."

"I wanted to find out more about Angelica Clayton's husband," Slocum said.

"You were digging into business that isn't none of your damn business," snapped the marshal. "You steer clear of the Iron-Silver Mining Company and their union trouble. There's enough brewin' on that horizon to keep me busy for a month of Sundays. I don't need you pokin' your nose in too."

"You think those three came all the way from Leadville just to kill the officers of the company?" Slocum asked, as if he hadn't heard the marshal's warning.

"I don't want you stirring up any more trouble. I think it's time you were moving on."

Slocum nodded. He'd been thinking along the same lines. There wasn't much more he could do in this city, especially since Linette had left.

"By morning," the marshal added. "I want you gone by tomorrow morning."

"Got some belongings to store. Mind if I tend to that before I leave?"

"The hotel's got the facilities. Just talk to them. I don't want to see your face in my town again." The marshal got to his feet and waddled off, his bowlegs even more obvious from the back.

The marshal may have cut a ludicrous figure, but Slocum knew that strong pressure had been brought on him. He didn't seem the kind to buckle without damn good reason.

Slocum paid his bill and left, going to the front desk to arrange for the storage of Linette's clothing. For two dollars in coin they'd keep it for six months. Slocum decided that this would be long enough. Either she returned for them or she didn't. He'd done what he could. Finished with this task, he went for a walk to settle his dinner and to help him think.

An hour's wandering through the city convinced him of his course of action. He was disappointed that Linette hadn't come to see him in the doctor's office or at least waited before taking off on her wild-goose chase. But he wasn't going to let the matter drop.

Not even considering Linette and her dead sister, he had a score to settle. Someone had tried to kill him, and he wasn't going to let that go unavenged.

Decided on what he should do, he returned and packed his gear. Sleep came slowly that night, and when it finally did arrive, Slocum tossed and turned restlessly. Before sunrise he was up and checked out of the Palmer House. In twenty minutes he had found the stage office.

He rubbed two gold half-eagles together as he waited for the clerk to finish with his invoices and sell him a ticket.

"Where to, mister?" the clerk finally asked.

"Leadville."

The clerk looked up as if someone had stuck him with a needle. "You don't have the look of a miner about you," he said uncertainly. Slocum thought of a rabbit wanting to run from a coyote. The clerk was mighty spooked over a simple ticketing request.

"There's more'n miners in a boomtown like Leadville, isn't there?"

"Yes, sir, of course there is. Here's your ticket. Stage leaves in twenty minutes. You can wait out on the platform or you can go next door to the café for coffee."

"Thanks," Slocum said, tossing his gear onto a pile waiting for the stagecoach. He felt the clerk's eyes boring holes in his back. Slocum thought about the brief exchange and decided there were two types of men going to Leadville.

The first dug in the ground and risked their lives to bring out silver ore. The second kind made their living with six-shooters. If the clerk knew he wasn't a miner, that left only gunfighter as a likely profession.

As he went to the café next door, Slocum reached over and unhooked the leather thong from the hammer of his Colt Navy. He had no good reason for being ready for a fight, but he had learned during the war to listen to his instincts. They'd kept him alive throughout some hard times.

For whatever reason, his instincts were screaming that trouble lay just ahead.

Several men worked on breakfast. A door at the rear of the small café led to the outhouse. Slocum settled down on a hard wooden stool near the front of the room and ordered coffee. It was bitter and almost as thick as mud, but it went a long way to driving away the fog in his head. Not getting enough sleep was a poor way to start a tedious trip into the high mountains.

Slocum had almost finished his coffee when the door at the rear opened and a man came in, still buttoning up his pants from doing his business out back. Slocum's cold green eyes locked with the man's, and time came to a halt for both of them.

The florid man was the one to break the tableau. He turned and ran back through the door, almost knocking it from its creaking hinges. Slocum took off after him, more to satisfy his curiosity than for any other reason.

The man had been the loser in the poker game the night before Angelica Clayton's wedding. What had twisted his conscience so bad that he'd turned tail and run at the mere sight of John Slocum?

Slocum went through the back door, then grew cautious. Bulling ahead was likely to get him killed. He rested his hand on the butt of his six-shooter, then advanced toward the outhouse. From the half dozen paths running to it, Slocum realized that the outhouse was used by more than just the café patrons. He ducked down and looked under the door. Wherever the man had gone, he hadn't sought refuge in the outhouse.

Slocum considered letting the matter drop. What was the man to him? Then his curiosity started getting the better of him. There wasn't any reason for the man to flee as he'd done.

Unless he thought Slocum knew about something the ruddy-complexioned man had done.

Losing wasn't enough to cause such a strong reaction. Slocum began wondering if the escaping man had anything to do with the killings at Angelica's wedding.

He dropped to one knee and studied the soft, damp dirt around the outhouse. Tracks slightly deeper than some of the others showed on one path. Slocum decided this had to have been caused by a man running, bringing his weight down hard in his effort to put as much distance between him and his pursuer as possible. Slocum paced along, checking the length of stride. Each boot mark was a good four feet apart. The man had definitely hit the ground running.

He headed on along the path marked with the heavy boot marks. Within two minutes Slocum slowed. A smile crossed his lips. Ahead was an alley littered with crates from a warehouse. The tracks led directly to an overturned wood box.

Slocum cocked his six-shooter and took careful aim. He squeezed off a round into the side of the box. Splinters flew everywhere, and a soft moan sounded. Only then did he advance.

Slocum almost died because he had underestimated his quarry.

A bullet ripped through the brim of his hat. Slocum jerked back instinctively and hit the ground, rolling over and over.

He fetched up hard against the wall of the warehouse. Pain shot through him from his injured ribs. This agony forced him to action. He'd know more than pain if he didn't make the right decisions—fast.

The crate had been a clever ruse. He saw that now. From the angle of the bullet, his adversary had claimed the high ground. Slocum lifted his pistol and fired.

This time the grunt that came was backed with the discharge of a pistol. Slocum got his feet under him and saw a man lying across a second-story windowsill. Slocum looked around to see if the brief exchange of gunfire had attracted attention. It hadn't. They weren't far from the stage depot and the railhead. Heavy wagons moved constantly in the street, their rattle and clank adding to the hiss of steam engines and the neighing of horses.

Slocum warily approached the crate he had thought was the man's hiding place and turned it over. The box had been used as a convenient stepping-stone to get into the warehouse. The florid man hadn't even paused here, much less used it as a hideout.

Slocum climbed onto the crate and reached up to grab the man's collar. The ruddy-complected man stirred a bit and moaned low as he hung in the broken window. Slocum heaved, bringing the man entirely out of the warehouse. He made no effort to hold him as he fell heavily to the alley below.

Jumping down, Slocum kept his would-be ambusher covered.

"Why'd you run like that?" Slocum asked. The man moaned softly but didn't move. Slocum kicked him in the ribs to get an answer. The only reply was a more guttural sound, this time not even a wail of pain. Slocum tried to place it; it was a gurgling noise.

Slocum rolled the man over and saw that the bullet had taken him just below the throat, and he was drowning in his own blood. Slocum stared at the man and wondered what the hell was going on. This was without doubt the loser from the poker game the night before Angelica's wedding. What gave him a guilty conscience and the need to run when he spotted Slocum in the café?

Reaching down, Slocum pulled out the man's wallet and flipped it open. There were a few greenbacks but no identification. Slocum continued to rummage in the wallet and found a small slip of paper. Holding it up to the sunlight, he made out the faded words that had been penciled on it.

He read a series of numbers. For a moment Slocum struggled to understand what it meant and why the man thought enough to keep it in his wallet. Then it hit Slocum like a sledgehammer blow.

The scrap of paper gave the date and time of Angelica Clayton's wedding.

He stared at the paper as if it would tell him more than he saw, then held it up to the morning sun. Part of a watermark came through, showing that the instructions for murder had been written on bonded paper. Slocum slipped it into his shirt pocket, then tossed the wallet back onto the ground beside the dying man. A few minutes earlier Slocum might have scouted up a doctor for the man.

Not now. Not knowing his victim had played a part in killing three men and Angelica Clayton.

Slocum spun and stalked off, returning to the depot just as the stagecoach pulled in. He lounged on the covered porch, watching the driver change teams. It was a long way into the Rockies, across Mosquito Pass, and down into Leadville.

Slocum knew what he was leaving behind in Denver. He wondered what he would find in the mining town.

5

Slocum thought he was going to die. The rough stagecoach ride over the mountain passes had jostled and banged and twisted him until his injured side was afire. A preacher man riding in the seat opposite him had taken pity and passed over a small flask with cheap whiskey in it. Slocum hadn't wanted to drink all the parson's liquor, but he found it hard to restrain himself.

The pain was almost more than he could stand.

"You're looking mighty pale, if I might be so bold to say it, sir," the preacher said, taking back the empty flask. "Is there anything I can do to ease your journey?"

"Nothing," Slocum said. The only good aspect of having to endure the torture of his wounded side was not dwelling on Linette or what he might find in Leadville.

The woman had gone somewhere. It must have been Leadville. Everything Slocum found about the killings pointed to the boomtown. Even the odd occurrence of the man running out of the café next to the stagecoach depot showed that answers to his questions were locked within the boundaries of the thriving mining town.

43

"I'm going to Leadville to start a congregation," the reverend said. "It is supposed to be a . . . dangerous town."

"Reckon there's more'n a few killings there," Slocum said. He looked at the somber man and remembered the response he had gotten from the clerk in the stagecoach office. Only two types of men went to Leadville: miners and killers.

The minister cleared his throat.

"My business there doesn't have anything to do with killing," Slocum said, lying as the words slipped from his mouth. He appreciated the minister's whiskey, but he didn't want to get him started on a drawn-out sermon on the evils of violence.

"There's considerable union unrest," the man said. "You don't have a hand in that, do you?"

"I don't work for either the miner's union or the Iron-Silver Mining Company." Slocum watched a flood of relief pass over the man's face.

"That's good."

"I'm looking for a woman," Slocum said suddenly. "She might have preceded me to Leadville by two or three days." Even as he spoke, he knew he'd made a mistake. If there were two kinds of men going to Leadville, there was only one kind of woman. The reverend got fired up about harlots and the sins of the flesh.

Slocum listened for a few seconds, then simply stared out the stagecoach's window. The canvas flap snapped in the wind and a steady storm of dust hit Slocum in the face. It was better than hearing about soiled doves.

The driver snapped a long whip and began pushing the team of six horses to their limit. Slocum strained to get the dirt from his eyes and saw why. Leadville was in sight. The driver and armed guard up in the box next to him had switched teams five times during the trip—but they hadn't even slept. They saw the end of a long, tiring journey, and to hell with the horses.

Slocum didn't like seeing animals abused, but he had to agree with the driver's longing to get out of the stagecoach. Listening to the preacher man was wearing real thin.

"Thank you, sir, for being so understanding," the reverend said as Slocum carefully dropped out of the coach and onto solid ground. "If I can find a dozen more like you in Leadville, my congregation will flourish."

"Good luck," Slocum said, not meaning it. He had no idea what drove men like this. He was trying to bring a touch of civilization to a town that didn't want it. Leadville had 116 saloons, 118 casinos, and 40,000 hard-drinking, whoring hard-rock miners who cared more for tying one on than eternal salvation.

After a twelve-hour shift five hundred feet underground, Slocum wasn't sure that they didn't have the right idea.

Slocum heaved his gear onto his shoulder and staggered under the load. He had to find a place to rest. Getting shot up hadn't done him any good, and he felt weaker than a newborn kitten. He walked along Chestnut Avenue looking for a decent place to stay. He found several, all filled. Slocum finally settled on a small, dingy place at the edge of town that charged more for one night than he'd paid in Denver at the luxurious Palmer House for three.

This was the reality of life in a boomtown. Everything cost too damn much.

"That's in advance," the unshaven room clerk said. "And it's twice that if you want your horse put up for the night."

"Don't have a horse," Slocum said. "And if I did, at these prices I'd let the horse sleep in the room with me. It'd be cheaper."

The clerk grunted and accepted Slocum's greenbacks with ill grace. He'd've preferred hard coin, but Slocum wasn't about to pass over any of his gold change. He might find places in Leadville that wouldn't accept scrip.

"Where do the boys from the Iron-Silver Mining Company drink?" Slocum asked.

"Try the Pioneer Club Saloon," the clerk said, looking at him strangely. Slocum grunted his thanks and dragged his gear up the stairs to the tiny room, almost filled to overflowing with a squalid, lice-infested bed. He dropped his saddle on the bed, vowing to use his bedroll and sleep on the floor when he got back.

Before he left, he tended his injuries again. To his surprise the wounds hadn't ripped open during the rough stagecoach journey to Leadville. He gingerly prodded the furrows where the buckshot had ripped him open and decided he was healing just fine. There'd be four long scars on his side, but they weren't the first he'd picked up. With luck he'd live long enough to pick up more.

Slocum left the hotel and walked slowly down Chestnut. The avenue brimmed with miners, either drunk and/or getting there fast. He avoided several as they wobbled and staggered. As he went, he kept his eyes peeled for a likely place to start asking questions. Most people in a frontier town like this didn't cotton much to a stranger asking questions. Slocum knew he'd have to tread lightly.

He snorted, and hot plumes of breath condensed in the cold night air. He'd have to be very careful when asking about the Iron-Silver Mining Company's business. He'd almost been run out of Denver by the federal marshal for his interest. His reception in Leadville wasn't likely to be any less emphatic.

Slocum went into one nameless saloon, and no one caring about this lack. From the look of the dust falling off their canvas clothing, the miners had just come off a shift at some silver mine. Slocum said nothing, preferring to stand in one corner and just listen to the ebb and flow of their rough conversation.

Most wasn't of any interest to him. The men bragged about the number of whores they'd bedded, the amount of liquor they'd drunk, and the tons of ore they'd drilled and blasted during their shift. But one man, whose voice carried above the others, caught Slocum's attention.

"The mine's the best the company's got, I tell you," the miner was saying. "We blow it and the Iron-Silver Mining Company will shut down. They'll turn to dust and blow away in the wind. That'd show 'em!"

He got argument from two others. Slocum wasn't sure what their point was. All agreed they were underpaid by the company, but no one seemed to have any definite ideas about how to collect more.

Slocum drank the watered-down whiskey and listened and thought. This hardly sounded like a hotbed of union activity. If anything, it was just the opposite. No one was able to agree on what they ought to do or what was fair pay for their backbreaking work.

"You're new around here," said a miner not five feet from Slocum. The miner lifted his shot glass in Slocum's direction and knocked back the amber contents. He made a face and motioned to the barkeep for another. Slocum indicated that he'd pay for the miner's drink but didn't want another himself.

"That's right neighborly," the miner said, staring into the murky liquor in his glass. "Not many in these parts have such charity in their souls." He sipped at the whiskey, made a face again, then added, "Not many even have souls."

"All sold out to the Iron-Silver Mining Company?" Slocum asked.

"You may be new in town, but you know what's happening."

"Tell me about it," Slocum said.

The miner hesitated, looked at his free drink, then settled against the bar, as if preparing himself for a long stay. Slocum tried to figure how much liquor it'd take before the man's tongue was entirely loose and flapping at both ends. The man was short, stocky, and had the look of a deep miner about him. The pasty expression and burn marks showed he spent most of his waking hours underground— or in a saloon—and those underground were occupied with blasting.

"It's nothing out of the ordinary. They're screwin' us something royal, and all we do is bend over for more."

"I heard rumors of union trouble."

"Where'd you hear bullshit like that? There's not a union worth a bucket of warm spit around here. Most couldn't get ten men out for a meeting, 'less they offered free booze and whores. Leadville's a mine-owner's paradise."

"And for the miner?" prodded Slocum.

The miner shrugged. "Sometimes it ain't so bad." He smiled and showed a series of gold teeth. Slocum got the miner's drift. A good miner kept his eyes open for small nuggets that just happened to go into pockets or mouths and got past the mine inspectors. Paying off the company inspectors wasn't unheard of, either. A good day of slipping gold dust into a pocket—or even one good nugget—might add a hundred dollars to a miner's pay.

It was thieving, pure and simple, but Slocum saw nothing wrong with it. The owners wouldn't miss it, and it might mean the difference between life and death for many of the miners.

"What's it like now?"

"Can't rightly say. We've been paid real good lately, but there's something going on."

"Above ground?"

"Yep." The miner waited for another drink before he

elaborated. "There's trouble brewing in the home office, if you ask me."

"Labor trouble?"

"Nobody cares a whit for that. This is between the owners, if you ask me. Or then, it might just be my imagination. I ain't got a whole lot to think about when I'm not blasting with five hundred feet of rock over my head."

"Bet you think about women," Slocum said, changing his tack. He had to listen to the miner's litany of woes, of how there just weren't that many women to go around in Leadville. Slocum had heard it all before. Men came to work and often to die. The only women likely to come this way were the saloon whores. Families always found it hard going with such primitive—and expensive—conditions.

"Any new ones come to Leadville?" Slocum asked when the miner ran down. The man was getting tipsy and his words were slurring. Slocum wasn't sure how much more he could get from him before he passed out entirely.

"Always a new one or two. Went down to the stagecoach to see if any came in this time. None did, dammit."

"How about in the past week or so? I'm real partial to dark-haired women myself." Slocum noticed he was starting to feel the effects of the liquor. He put it off to the altitude more than to his weakness from the shotgunning at the wedding.

"Can't say I seen any come in. If'n they did, it might have been in one of the damned hoity-toity director's coaches. They're all the time coming in from Denver. No telling what goes on inside them posh stagecoaches."

The miner slumped, dropping to his knees and trying to support himself on the bar with his elbows. Slocum heaved him into a nearby chair and left the saloon, never looking back. The sharp, cold mountain air hit him like a blow to the face. The trace of drunkenness that had been dulling his senses inside was erased by the wind.

He shivered and pulled his jacket tighter around him. He needed rest, but something drove him on. He remembered what the room clerk had said about the Pioneer Club Saloon. It took a bit of asking, but Slocum finally found it at the far end of town, near the road leading to the Colorado Prince Mine. The darkness falling on Leadville was almost absolute by the time he reached the end of the street. Slocum had gotten used to the streetlights in Denver and the bright, shining glow from hundreds of windows. Most in Leadville were dark, either from lack of lamp oil or exhausted sleep.

Slocum stared at the exterior of the Pioneer Club Saloon and knew it was a ritzier place than the other, where he'd pumped the willing, thirsty miner for information. The club was in a three-story brick building. Slocum circled the structure, studying the layout. A quiet hotel was connected by a third-story walkway, giving access without the need to come to street level. This told Slocum more about the club's patrons than anything else.

Only the rich need try to drink at the Pioneer Club Saloon.

Walking to the closed front door, Slocum peered through the etched glass window. Just inside stood a large man— the gatekeeper. If he didn't like a patron's looks, this was as far as he got. Slocum saw a wide, wooden staircase curling up to the second floor.

He decided he had nothing to lose. He entered and immediately found his way blocked by the man-mountain of mean muscle.

"Private club, sir," the bouncer said. His words were polite, but he growled deep in his throat like a riled grizzly.

"I'm looking for a friend of mine," Slocum said. "You might know her."

"There's plenty of women down the street. Try the cribs over on Elm Street."

"That's not the kind of woman I was looking for. My friend's name is Linette Clayton."

Slocum watched the man's expression closely. There wasn't even a flicker of recognition.

"This *is* the Pioneer Club Saloon? She was supposed to meet me here tonight. Fact is, I'm a mite late meeting her. Don't want to get her mad at me."

"The name's right for the club. But I don't know any woman by that name around here."

"Mind if I just take a quick look inside?" Slocum tried to push past and found himself butting up against a solid wall of muscle.

"She's not here. You don't get in without a membership or having a member with you."

"Thanks," Slocum said, backing off. He wasn't in any shape to press the issue. From the look of the Pioneer Club Saloon, he guessed that this was exactly the type of place Linette would come if she was bent on revenge.

Rich men whiled away their idle hours here, rich men with information about who'd be responsible for the death of Angelica Clayton. Even more important for Linette, the same men would have the power to do something about it.

Slocum looked at the club over his shoulder as he returned to his more humble hotel. A shiver passed through him, and it wasn't from the chill wind blowing off the Rockies.

6

Slocum slept until the sun rose over the Rockies. He stirred and sneezed. The cold in the room had worked its way into his bones. He stretched and moaned as his side protested. Rubbing his wound gently, he got the circulation flowing. Only then did he get his feet over the edge of the bed and onto the freezing floor.

Most of Leadville had been at work for hours. The mountains being where they were, only a few lucky ones ever got to go to work in sunlight until the middle of June. And even then the mornings were cut short compared with Denver.

This was fine with Slocum. He preferred roaming the night-cloaked town's streets. It was more dangerous—and it was also a time when he felt more alive.

He found a small, clean café and ate, wincing at the high cost of the food. Ten dollars for a breakfast would have brought out pistols and sent lead flying had any restaurant in Denver tried to charge it. But not in Leadville. Here, not getting poisoned with tainted food was worth the expense.

Slocum finished the simple meal and started a more careful search for Linette.

After four hours of looking, he gave up the hunt. She had come to Leadville. Her note hinted at that much. But where was she? Had she been killed by the men she sought in her sister's death? Slocum cursed her headstrong behavior. She never should have rushed off without seeing him first. Even though he'd been badly shot up, he could have helped her back in Denver.

Here? He wasn't sure he could do a damn thing for the woman.

Slocum snorted in disgust. He wasn't even having any luck *finding* her, much less helping her bring some decent frontier justice to her sister's murderers.

"Good day, pilgrim," came a cheery voice. Slocum saw the preacher man who had ridden with him from Denver. He tipped his hat and tried to keep walking. The preacher matched his step. "We seem to be going the same way," the parson said.

"I doubt that," Slocum said. "I was hunting for a decent bar to get drunk in." He knew of no other way of getting rid of the unwanted attention given him by the preacher.

"Demons swim in whiskey," the preacher said solemnly. "A touch keeps the body warm and alert. Too much drowns our senses and opens our hearts and minds to Satan's influence."

Slocum turned and looked at the man squarely. He seemed open and honest. Slocum wished he would go recruit for his church where it might do him more good. If things went well, Slocum didn't intend on staying in Leadville more than a few days.

And if things didn't go well, he'd be gone even sooner.

"Have you tried asking some of the mine owners for support?" Slocum asked. "They ought to be willing to pay a bit for someone wanting to look after the spiritual well-being of their miners."

"Why, no, the thought never occurred to me."

"Then we might be going the same way," Slocum said. "Come on. Let's go see what can be done over at the Pioneer Club Saloon. I'm sure quite a few of the mine owners are there."

Slocum's mind raced as he strode along beside the preacher. The man rattled on about his high-flying hopes and plans. Slocum ignored most of what was said, nodding occasionally and encouraging him to keep talking. Slocum didn't want the burden of keeping up his end of the conversation. His mind was already racing ahead to getting into the Pioneer Club Saloon and what he might accomplish once inside.

"Such a fine building," the preacher said. "And the hotel next to it is certainly finer than most in Leadville. At least it's better than the ones I've had occasion to visit."

Slocum opened the door for the preacher. A different bouncer came up.

"Peace, brother," the preacher said. "My friend and I have come to speak with—"

"Those willing to help a man of the cloth establish his church in Leadville," Slocum said, not knowing any names to use to gain entry. "The reverend here knows they won't turn down his request."

Slocum saw a hint of intelligence in this bouncer's eyes. He wasn't as large as the other—and Slocum guessed he was even more dangerous if crossed. This was a man with both deadly fists and a cunning mind.

"Wait here for a moment, gentlemen," he said. Slocum edged into the lobby and peered around a corner into a sitting room. The bouncer spoke softly to a well-dressed man seated at a large table with four other men. Even though the bouncer interrupted their poker game, none seemed upset. Slocum had seen this before.

Among their own kind, rich men didn't mind losing. It was only when they gambled with inferiors and lost did their ire rise. Then they became implacable opponents, willing to cheat and even to kill.

"Come in, gentlemen. Mr. Conrad will speak to you. He's the general manager of the club."

Slocum let the reverend precede him. He suddenly realized he hadn't the slightest idea what the preacher's name was. He had been more interested in using him as a way to gain entry than in anything he had to say about salvation.

The manager took in the preacher's shabby clothing and manner and came to immediate decisions. His gaze lingered somewhat longer on Slocum, as if he were trying to figure out why he was there.

"Preacher, if you're going to be a while, why don't I just go upstairs for a spell?" Slocum said. He didn't think either the bouncer or the manager would say no.

And he was right. Conrad pointed to a chair where the preacher sat, hands on knees, as he earnestly told the man the benefits of having a decent church established in Leadville. The bouncer followed Slocum, watching silently as he went up the stairs.

The downstairs had been posh. Upstairs was even more richly appointed. Slocum had been in places rivaling the Pioneer Club Saloon before, but that had been in San Francisco's Union Club. He hadn't expected such luxury in a mining boomtown like Leadville.

Slocum looked around the room. A half dozen men, all well dressed, drank from cut-crystal glasses. The only exceptions he saw were two men huddled together at a back table. Although they weren't roughly dressed like miners, they did not belong in such sumptuous surroundings. Slocum sat in an alcove near them.

"Sir, what is your pleasure?" asked the waiter. Slocum had seen the look pass between the barkeep and the bouncer, still standing at the head of the polished wood stairs. It had been a small nod, but significant. It established that Slocum belonged here.

"Brandy," he said. The waiter drifted away, his feet hardly seeming to move as he went to the long teakwood bar to place the order with the barkeep.

Slocum savored the wealth of this fancy club. It was the kind of place that both drew and repelled him. The money that changed hands in card games and in other ways was a powerful pull for him, but the tycoons who wielded the power and the money weren't his type of men—and they weren't likely to have any dealings with his kind, either.

He leaned back when the brandy arrived and sipped at it. He wasn't surprised when he found that it was real. He had ordered French brandy on a Mississippi riverboat once and had gotten nitric acid and charred peach pits soaked in alcohol. But this brandy burned the mouth and throat and settled peacefully in his belly. Slocum knew he could learn to enjoy a life with such fine liquor in it.

The men at the table behind him spoke in guarded whispers. As he studied the half dozen others in the room, he half listened. A single sentence alerted him.

". . . never showed up. He was supposed to be on the stage yesterday."

"What could have happened to the son of a bitch?" asked the second man. "He's usually more dependable than this. Think it's a whore he found in Denver?"

"I doubt it. His prick's about ready to fall off from the clap. I'm going to tell the boss that he might have gotten nabbed."

"By who?" the first said scoffingly. "The marshal couldn't find his ass with both hands."

"Might be the owl hoot who shot me."

Slocum almost reached for his six-shooter and opened up again. He had blundered across two of the men who had shot up Angelica Clayton's wedding. If he had killed the third in Denver, he could have all their heads in one quick flash of gunfire.

He held himself in check. They had said they worked for someone else. He remembered the slip of paper he had taken off the florid-faced man in Denver, too. That was a written order from someone well heeled. Slocum would be happy putting a slug through each of their putrid hearts, but he wanted the man who had ordered the attack on the wedding party. Only then could he feel he had been successful.

And he still had no idea what had become of Linette. He damned himself for being a fool, but she mattered.

The two men rose and walked out, still talking quietly to each other. Slocum caught one parting comment.

"We can still ambush him—" The rest of the bush-whacker's words vanished when the barkeep dropped a glass.

Slocum finished his brandy, then reached into his vest pocket to find the money to cover it. The waiter glided up to him and put both hands in front of his chest, as if he were surrendering.

"It's on the house, sir."

"That's real hospitable," Slocum said, distracted by the two men making their way down the stairs. He heard the front doors slam. They had left on their mission, probably to kill someone else. They had been keyed-up, and the one had repeatedly glanced at the huge Regulator clock on the wall. Slocum had taken part in enough holdups to recognize the nervous gestures.

These two had waited for their partner, maybe the one Slocum had left dead back in the Denver alley. When he didn't show up, they had to spring their trap and kill again.

At least that was the way Slocum read their actions. He

knew he might be wrong, but he didn't think so. He tipped his hat in the direction of two men drinking at a table across the room, then hurried down the stairs.

"Sir" came the cold voice of the club's manager. Slocum turned to Conrad.

"Has the preacher left already? I'm sorry to have missed him like this," Slocum said, wanting to get on the two men's trail.

"We've come to an understanding that might be mutually profitable," Conrad said. "Thank you for bringing him by." Conrad glanced at the bouncer. Slocum didn't see the signal that passed between them. The manager reached into his vest pocket and handed Slocum a small golden medallion.

"What's this?" Slocum asked.

"A membership in the Pioneer Club Saloon. You've earned it." Conrad turned and went back to his card game in the parlor. Slocum stared at the medallion, then put it into his pocket. He wondered what had gone on between the preacher and Conrad, then pushed it from his mind. He had more important matters to tend to.

He rushed into the street and looked back toward the center of Leadville. Two clouds of dust marked where horses' hooves had cut up the hard-packed street. Slocum cursed under his breath. He hadn't been thinking too clearly. He ought to have arranged for a horse when he'd gotten here. Now he had to find a livery and dicker the best he could. The two owl hoots he was after might be halfway to Denver before he found a decent horse.

Slocum stopped and stared at a man just dismounting in front of a saloon a dozen yards down the street from the Pioneer Club Saloon. He raced to the man and said, "I'll give you ten dollars if I can borrow your horse for an hour."

"What?" The man stared at him as if he were crazy. Slocum glanced over his shoulder. The dust clouds were slowly being blown away. In another few minutes he wouldn't be able to figure out where the two men had gone.

"Twenty dollars."

"That horse is *expensive*," the man insisted. "It cost me a young fortune."

"I just want to rent it, not buy it. Twenty dollars."

"In gold?"

Slocum fumbled and found a double eagle and passed it over. The man bit it, let the sun reflect off the shiny surface, then nodded.

With a bound Slocum swung into the saddle. "You going to be here a while?" he called.

"Reckon so."

"I'll be back in an hour—two at the most—to return the horse."

The man laughed. Slocum put his heels to the animal's flanks. The old horse faltered and almost balked. He had to coax it into a steady gait. From the canter he was able to get a dispirited gallop out of it. The horse wasn't fit for a glue factory, much less twenty dollars in gold, but Slocum wasn't in any position to complain.

He slowed to a trot and then reined in when he got to the other end of Leadville. The road branched. He was certain the men he was following had come this way. But which road had they taken? One led into Mosquito Pass and over to Denver. The other went up into the hills. A sign marked LITTLE PITTSBURGH MINE was stuck crookedly in the hard ground on the other side of the road. Slocum tried to figure why they'd want to return to Denver.

There wasn't any good reason. It struck him as more likely that his targets had ridden the trail to the Little Pittsburgh Mining Company claim. He didn't hesitate putting his heels to the horse's bony flanks, urging it to more speed than it probably had achieved in years.

The horse began to tire quickly, forcing Slocum to rein

back. But he got a chance to study the dusty road more now, and saw small clues that the pair had recently passed by. Shiny nicks in the rock gleamed in the sun. An occasional spot looked to be recently disturbed. The trail might belong to anyone, but Slocum didn't think so.

He pulled to a stop when he saw how the road began curling around on itself. This was the perfect spot for an ambush. Slocum dismounted and climbed to the top of a rise. From this vantage point he could see the bending road well. In the far distance, past the Little Pittsburgh Mine, rose a dust cloud. Someone was approaching slowly.

It took Slocum a few minutes to find where the two men had set up their ambush. He had to hand it to them. They knew their job. One had taken a rifle and crawled up onto a boulder on the left side of the road. The other had remained on the right side of the road, using a small stand of scrub oak for cover. They could catch anyone on the road in a devastating cross fire.

This wasn't Slocum's fight, but he wasn't going to let those murdering cayuses strike again. A rattler might get one hit; Slocum wasn't the kind of man to let it bite a second time.

He pulled out his Colt Navy, wishing he had his own gear. His trusty Winchester could drop both the bushwhackers, even at this range. But he had to get closer. He made sure the horse was safely tethered, then started down the rocky slope, intent on sneaking up behind the man in the oak grove.

"Here he comes," warned the man, sprawled belly-down on the boulder. "You ready, Harry?"

"All ready," called the other backshooter, not ten feet in front of Slocum.

Slocum's plan was simple enough. He was going to creep up on the one called Harry, coldcock him, then move on the other. With the rifle he intended to get in the attack, he could take on the man atop the boulder.

Nothing went right.

Just as Slocum was covering the last few feet between him and Harry, the man spun, rifle leveled. What warned him, Slocum couldn't say. All he knew was that something had spooked the man—and a finger was tensing around a rifle trigger.

Slocum got off the first shot. It went wild, ricocheting off a rock. This frightened Harry and gave Slocum the chance for a second and more accurate shot. It took Harry high in the chest. The man rocked back, then simply sat down, a stupid look on his face.

Slocum found himself on the receiving end of a fusillade of bullets from the other man. All hope for secrecy had fled. Slocum fired at the bushwhacker, but he was out of range and didn't have a clear shot, even if he had had a rifle.

He dodged the best he could, emptied his six-shooter, then reloaded. By this time the man he'd shot had regained his senses and crawled into the brush. Slocum wished he'd had the chance to finish him off. There wasn't any real evidence, but he was sure this had been one of the men who had shot up Angelica Clayton's wedding.

"Get the hell out of here!" came the cry from behind the boulder across the road.

Slocum tried to target the voice. He fired a few times and then stopped, conserving his ammunition.

The rattle of the carriage coming down the road made Slocum spin. The carriage driver was reining in. The scene flashed in Slocum's head. He saw the man on the boulder rising. He heard the rifle's report. The driver jerked to one side, then fell into the box.

Slocum used his last three shots to drive the gunman back to cover.

Then the carriage rattled by, out of control.

7

Slocum reacted instinctively rather than thought about what he was doing. He slid his Colt into its cross-draw holster and leapt. His hand tangled in the dangling leather reins of the runaway carriage's team. He was dragged for several yards before he got his feet under him. A frightened horse turned and stared at him, white showing in a stark rim around the brown eye.

He yanked back hard, pulling the horse's head down. This caused the animal to break stride. Slocum used the stumbling to get his own balance. He was running easily now. He threw his arm around the horse's neck as if he were bulldogging it. The other horse broke stride and slowed. A hard turn and he had the animal stopped.

Slocum gathered the reins and walked back to the carriage. He was sweating from the exertion and knew his jacket had seen its finest days. It hung in tatters from his shoulders. Worst of all, he had wrenched his healing wounds. Sharp needles of pain danced along his ribs.

He glanced into the driver's box and saw how much worse it could have been. The man was dead. The ambusher's bullet hadn't killed him outright but had cut an important artery. Without checking closer, Slocum thought the bullet had gone through the driver's neck. He had bled to death in minutes.

"You won't get anything from me!" came the cry from inside the carriage. For an instant Slocum thought it belonged to a woman. When the passenger got his fright under control, his voice lowered enough for Slocum to change his guess as to the occupant's sex.

"It's all right," Slocum said. "I shot one and drove the other bushwhacker off. Your driver's dead, though."

"Alfred?"

A man's head poked through the carriage's side curtain. He wore a stylish top hat, and velvet tabs on his foppish coat gleamed in the hot Colorado sun.

"If that's his name," Slocum said.

"Damnation! What's this country coming to!" The man piled out of the carriage, eyeing Slocum. He thrust out a hand that had never seen a day's work. Slocum shook it cautiously.

"I thank you profusely, sir. You have come to my aid when I needed it most. How ever may I reward you?"

"There's no need," Slocum said, his mind racing. "After all, it's only what one gentleman would do for another." He glanced down at his battered jacket. "My clothing is a bit tattered from the gunfight. I apologize for that."

Slocum had gauged his words well. The man looked like a flower blossoming in the warm spring sunlight.

"It is so refreshing to meet a man of breeding. These awful barbarians!"

"I happened to be riding along, going toward the Little Pittsburgh Mine, when I saw the two men preparing their ambush. I didn't know who they were trying to dry-gulch, so I waited. They opened fire on you when you came into range," Slocum said, changing important details to make his own part seem all the more heroic.

"A fine coincidence it is, too," the man said, brushing the dust off his already spotless clothing.

"Coincidence?"

"You were riding up to the mine and I was riding into Leadville. You see, sir, I am the owner of the Little Pittsburgh Mining Company." He coughed politely. "Rather, I am a major shareholder in the company. I do hold the controlling interest but do not own it outright. My name is Carter Stevenson."

Slocum thought he was going to whip off his hat and perform a deep bow from the waist. He stopped just short of such a courtly action. Slocum introduced himself.

"Allow me to buy you a drink. I should think your whistle would need wetting, eh?"

Slocum allowed as to how he had worked up a thirst. A thought came to him. "Allow me to take you to my club," he said. Slocum pulled out the membership medallion for the Pioneer Club Saloon and spun it in the air for Stevenson to see.

"A good club. Mr. Conrad runs a fine operation," said Stevenson, "But I must insist on buying."

Slocum detected just a bit of condescension in Stevenson's words. He wondered how this could be. The Pioneer Club Saloon was about the finest establishment Slocum had seen this side of San Francisco—and that included several choice saloons in Denver.

"The Leadville Trotting and Racing Club is *my* club," Stevenson said haughtily.

"An excellent club," Slocum said, never having heard of it. "I would be honored to be your guest." He paused, then asked Stevenson, "Can you manage to get back to Leadville? If you'd like, I can drive."

"Would you, Mr. Slocum? It has been years since I handled a team."

Slocum almost laughed. These two horses hardly counted as a "team." Any decent mule skinner would have eaten them for breakfast—and still been hungry.

"And I'd be most interested in knowing why you were going out to the mine."

Slocum heard the razor edge come into those words. Carter Stevenson might appear a fop, but he had a steel core to him. Slocum had almost underestimated him.

"If you'd direct me to the club, Mr. Stevenson, I'd be glad to discuss the matter with you." Slocum decided he could come up with a plausible reason for being on the road to the Little Pittsburgh mine by the time they reached Leadville.

"Certainly." Stevenson barked out the instructions as if Slocum were his driver rather than his savior. Slocum paid no attention to the imperious tones. He had the feeling Stevenson was part of the answer to what had happened at Angelica Clayton's wedding—and what had happened to Linette.

If the same men who had killed four at the wedding also wanted Stevenson dead, there had to be some connection. All he had to do was find it.

Slocum simply sat and stared. He knew the Pioneer Club Saloon was a posh place. Carter Stevenson's circle was even more elegant. The Leadville Trotting and Racing Club had velvet drapes and beaten gold-leaf plates for small food items Slocum couldn't begin to identify, and wine served from crystal decanters by silent waiters.

Slocum knew the place had more than simple elegance. No one batted an eye at his dishabille. Since he was with Stevenson, he had to be a gentleman. Slocum found himself uneasy, nonetheless.

"I tell you," Stevenson was saying, "this man's a hero! He saved me from those bushwhackers."

"Why were they trying to kill you, Carter?" asked one of the interested crowd circling Stevenson. "Didn't you give enough to charity this month?"

"You ought to give more," Stevenson grumbled. "There are starving men and decent women in Leadville. We have more than enough to share some of it."

"But not too much," the man retorted. This brought a general laugh from the crowd. Slocum saw Stevenson smile uneasily. The man might not be a saint—what mine owner was?—but he was closer than any of the others in the room.

"That's not the point," Stevenson said, steering the conversation back to his topic. "We're not safe riding along the roads in Leadville. We've got to do something about it to make it less dangerous."

"We can always buy a sheriff."

The suggestion fell on deaf ears. Slocum was interested in the men's reasoning. He worked on it, then decided that they could have their own private armies if there wasn't an elected sheriff. They were minor kings, each in his own domain. They made the law, and to hell with a democratically chosen sheriff.

"We ought to get the township to hire one," said Stevenson. "Let the townspeople who benefit from a sheriff pay for him."

"That's not going to keep you safe out on the road to your mine, Carter," said another. "A sheriff would have his hands full here in Leadville. We've got more saloons than any dozen sheriffs could keep quiet."

"There is always the chance of getting a federal marshal out to Leadville," suggested another. "We might get the government to send a marshal or two to guard our ore shipments. I've had three shipments to the Pueblo smelters hijacked this year."

"You have a dozen guards going with each shipment," said Stevenson. "A single marshal isn't going to change that." He let out a deep sigh. "It doesn't seem as if either an elected sheriff or a federal marshal is the answer, does it?"

"We're doing just fine, Carter. Let's not complicate the situation. Hell, I'm taking half a million a year in silver from just one small mine. All ten of my mines turn close to three million. And you're doing even better than that just from the Little Pittsburgh."

Slocum's ears pricked up at the numbers. He stared at Stevenson with new appreciation. The man wasn't just rich, he was *rich*. Any silver mine producing more than three million dollars a year was a bonanza.

The talk died down and the group broke up into smaller parties. Stevenson took Slocum by the arm and guided him to a private table with a view of the mountains from a large plate-glass window. They were on the fourth floor of the building, and Slocum felt above the cares of the world.

"This is my personal table," Stevenson said. "I enjoy sitting and staring at the mountains. The others have their mines in the hills, of course, but the Little Pittsburgh returns more than any three of them."

"You're a wealthy man. Is that why those two tried to kill you today?"

"They might have only wanted to kidnap me," said Stevenson. "Ransom can be considerable in these cases." He sounded as if he spoke from personal experience.

Slocum didn't know how much to tell the mine owner. Overhearing the two in the Pioneer Club Saloon had convinced him that they weren't simple highwaymen. They acted as if they had to follow a precise timetable—and one set forth for them by someone else. Just being allowed into the club meant they had powerful backers.

"Did they both escape?" asked Stevenson.

"I plugged one real good," said Slocum. "The other got away unscratched. But the one . . ." His voice trailed off as he tried to picture how bad the road agent's wound might have been. He had hit him square in the chest, up high. There hadn't been much blood, but Slocum didn't put much store in that.

"A shame. If even one had died or been left behind, I could have found out more." Stevenson smiled crookedly. "Money talks."

"I know," said Slocum. "It's said good-bye to me more than once."

Stevenson laughed at the small joke and turned to the plate of beef before him. Neither he nor Slocum had ordered. The waiter had simply brought the food. Slocum dug in with a passion. The succulent meat hardly needed a knife to cut it. The touch of a fork was enough to make it part. And when it reached his mouth, it dissolved in a burst of flavor that was better than anything Slocum had ever eaten.

It was an indication of how much money flowed through Leadville that a place like the Leadville Trotting and Racing Club could even exist.

"From the other side you can see the horse track," Stevenson said. "I do enjoy betting. Are you a gambling man, Mr. Slocum?"

"I've been known to place a bet or two," Slocum said.

"We can go out to the track sometime." Stevenson frowned. "How rude of me. I haven't inquired as to your business in Leadville. You are obviously not a laborer. And I have no illusion that you're a professional savior, riding a white steed and intent on coming to the aid of men beset by villains."

Again Slocum sensed the core of steel in Carter Stevenson. The man seemed almost scatterbrained at times, then did an about-face and showed how he had come by his considerable hoard of money. Slocum was a good judge of men. Whatever Carter Stevenson had, he had fought for and won through his own efforts.

"I'm looking for a friend," Slocum said, hoping Stevenson would let the explanation stand without elaboration. When the man started to ask more, Slocum cut him off, saying, "Looks as if I got to Leadville too late. He's already pushed on farther west. He never was one to stay around long."

"Why are you seeking this . . . friend?"

"He owes me a considerable sum of money," Slocum lied. He didn't know why he wasn't open with Stevenson. The man's enemies were Slocum's. "I'm not one to let a debt go unpaid."

Stevenson accepted this, since it had the ring of truth to it. Slocum didn't need to specify what the debt was. He straightened in the plush chair and felt his side give a twinge. That wound alone was reason enough to track the men to the ends of the earth.

Slocum was sure now that the man he'd killed in Denver, the one who had been in the poker game the night before the wedding, had been one of the killers. The other two rounded out those who had pulled the trigger on four people at Angelica's wedding. Slocum looked around the room. And was their boss among these wealthy mining tycoons?

If the two killers frequented the Pioneer Club Saloon, their employer might just be at home in a place like this.

Slocum looked out the window and saw the sunset turning the Rockies blood red. He took this as an omen. He'd find the men and their boss. The dry dust around Leadville would suck up their blood, and nobody would know or care.

Slocum turned, his sixth sense nudging him. He saw a woman spin suddenly and dash off in the direction of the kitchen. He had only a fleeting glimpse of her, but Slocum knew her.

Linette Clayton had just run from the room to keep him from seeing her. Slocum wanted to find out why.

8

"Excuse me a moment," Slocum said, pushing his chair back. It startled him when a waiter appeared out of nowhere to move the chair for him. He wasn't used to such attentive service.

"You look jumpy, Mr. Slocum. Is anything wrong? The service? The food? We can order something else, if you like."

"Nothing's wrong with the food or the service," Slocum said, intent on following Linette. "I'll be back in a few minutes." He had almost lost the two men when they'd left the Pioneer Club Saloon on their way to kill Stevenson. He had the feeling that if he lost Linette now, he might never find her again.

What worried him most was the feeling that the two who had ambushed Carter Stevenson might also kill her. He tried to shake off such nonsense but couldn't. It seemed as if everything in Leadville was tied together somehow—and he couldn't find the proper strand to follow to unravel it.

"What's down there?" he asked the maître d'. Slocum

eyed the doors leading off the narrow passage he thought
Linette had taken in her haste to avoid him.

"There are a few private rooms and our service area.
None is occupied at the moment," the man said. Slocum
saw how the maître d's jacket hung open—and why. The
butt of a small-caliber pistol poked out from under his left
arm. The help at the Leadville Trotting and Racing Club
was ready for any problem that might arise.

He looked over his shoulder at the men gathered in the
fourth-story dining room. Most he had seen when Stevenson
was giving his account of the attempted murder out on the
road. One or two had entered afterward, and he hadn't gotten
a good look at them. A corpulent, blustery-looking walrus
of a man sat at a corner table. From the way the room was
laid out, the tables at the corners near the windows were
reserved for only the wealthiest patrons.

Stevenson had one. So did the man with the big, bushy
mustache and huge potbelly.

"A friend of mine went down this corridor a few minutes
ago. I wanted to speak with her."

"I saw no one come this way," the maître d' said, spreading his hands expressively to show that Slocum was wel-
come to explore if he wanted. Slocum guessed that little
was off-limits to members of this club. Even their guests
received the same consideration.

Slocum started down the narrow passage, aware of how
trapped he would be if anything went wrong. His shoulders
brushed the walls on either side. He reached across and
slipped the thong off his Colt's hammer, trying to remember
if he had loaded five or six rounds into its cylinder after the
fight on the road. When he was traveling, he kept the hammer resting on an empty chamber as a safety measure. He
was beginning to think he might need the extra round.

He stopped when he came to tall swinging doors. Cautiously poking his head through, he looked around. Stairs

spiraled down from this preparation area to the kitchen on the ground floor. Tables littered with dirty dinner plates and wine goblets lined the walls. Slocum almost left when he saw a small piece of intricate white lace sticking out from under a closed door.

Walking on cat's feet, he went to the door, his hand still resting on the ebony handle of his six-shooter. He turned the knob slowly, then jerked open the door.

Linette Clayton stood inside the small linen closet. The hem of her dress had caught in the door as she'd closed it behind her.

"This isn't much of a hiding place," Slocum said. He didn't know what he felt. Anger ought to be at the forefront. It wasn't, not exactly. In spite of Linette's running off and leaving him in Denver, in spite of her turning tail and running from him to hide in the closet, he was still glad to see her.

"John, I didn't want you involved in this."

"I am," he said, relaxing a mite. There wasn't any call for him to draw down on her. He slipped the leather thong back over the six-shooter's hammer.

"You're looking fit," Linette said, her blue eyes dancing the way he remembered so well. "The gunshots aren't bothering you?"

"The doc back in Denver fixed me up pretty well," he said. "Why didn't you come by to see me?"

"I did!" Linette protested hotly. "I came by right after you were laid up. I looked in and—you looked like death. The doc wasn't so sure you'd pull through."

Slocum said nothing to this. He had been a bloody mess, but the doctor hadn't even hinted that the wounds were all that bad.

"I couldn't do anything for you," the raven-haired woman went on, "but I could do something about the terrible fiends who slaughtered Angelica and Rupert."

"You tracked them to Leadville?"

"I . . . not exactly," she said. Linette's eyes dropped to the floor, a child caught with her hand in the cookie jar. "I talked with some of the others in the Iron-Silver Mining Company. The three men killed at the wedding weren't the only officers who have been in danger. One, a vice president, has been shot at several times in the past month. Only luck has allowed him to live."

"So?" Slocum wasn't sure where this was leading.

"Don't you see? Someone is out to kill all the officers of the company Rupert worked for. I came to Leadville to meet with the president of the company."

Slocum heard more in the woman's words than she was telling him. More than this, something about a plot to kill all Iron-Silver Mining Company's officers worried at his gut. Slocum remembered hearing how several of the other mine owners had had trouble with bushwhackers—and how close the two men had come to killing Carter Stevenson.

"What have you found out?" Slocum asked.

"I—" Linette bit back the rest of her words. She spun around and started rummaging in the closet, knocking things onto the floor. "Wherever can those napkins be?" she said loudly.

Slocum turned and saw a man in the doorway. His hand went for his six-shooter. It was the man he had driven away with his gunfire, the one who had almost killed Stevenson.

Slocum could end this here and now. Angelica's killers would be brought to bloody justice, and to hell with the man who had hired them to do it.

"What's going on in there?" came an unpleasant, booming voice. The fat man Slocum had seen sitting at the table at the far side of the club dining room pushed past the hired killer in the doorway, using his potbelly to move the man out of his way. His dewlaps bounced as he shifted from one foot to the other, and he scowled so hard, his eyes vanished into pits of gristle.

"Linette, my darling, what's going on? Griff saw this man follow you back. Is everything all right?"

"Of course it is, Henry. Mr. Slocum was looking for the—"

"I was looking for a chamber pot," Slocum finished for Linette. "Been out all day and the pressure's building up. Not quite the thing to ask a lady, I know, but—"

"You're that friend of Carter's, aren't you?" The man waddled over, his huge bulk even more grotesque than Slocum had first thought. He stopped just short of banging his paunch against Slocum's rock-hard belly.

"I helped him out on the road today."

"Road agents, wasn't it?" The man's pig eyes narrowed to slits. Slocum felt as if he were being ripped apart by a buzzard, every piece studied before being devoured hungrily.

"Reckon so."

"I'm so rude," Linette said, hanging on to a pile of linen napkins she'd found in the closet. "This is Mr. Henry Hackett, the president and majority shareholder of the Colorado Prince."

"Finest mine in all Leadville district," Hackett said, his jowls bouncing as he spoke. "Even bigger producer than Carter's miserable Little Pittsburgh."

The man Hackett had called Griff moved to one side. Slocum saw his hand sliding under a fancy dress coat. With his own pistol in its cross-draw holster and secured with a thong, Slocum knew he'd stand no chance at all if Griff made a play. He wished he had his derringer with him. That would come to hand more easily out of a vest pocket than his six-shooter ever could from his holster.

"Get on back to the table, Linette," Hackett ordered. "Dinner's being served."

Slocum looked from Hackett to Griff. There was only hardness in Griff's eyes. He wasn't sure the man recognized him from the set-to out on the road, but it hardly mattered. Slocum knew a cold-blooded killer when he saw one. Griff would kill for the simple pleasure of it. He didn't need a reason.

As Linette passed in front of him, Slocum turned to one side and bumped her. The minor distraction allowed him to get his Colt Navy clear. He didn't draw it, but his hand rested on the ebony handle.

Linette seemed unaware of the deadly drama being played out around her. She smiled brightly and hurried off with the white linen napkins. Henry Hackett cleared his throat and spat on the floor, then turned and waddled after her, his ponderous girth entirely filling the narrow corridor.

Griff saw that the tide had turned against him. He had his hand on a hidden pistol; Slocum was ready to draw, too.

"You shot up a friend of mine today," Griff said. "I don't take kindly to that."

Slocum knew better than to retort. Griff might not know he was the man who'd been gunned down during Angelica's wedding. If he found that out, he might suspect Linette.

Slocum cursed his lack of knowledge. What the hell was Linette up to with Henry Hackett? Did she even know the mining magnate's henchman was responsible for her sister's death?

Slocum held a few hole cards, but he wasn't going to play them now. He was where Griff's influence was bigger than his. He certainly wasn't going to let them know he had also killed the man back in Denver at the stagecoach depot. Let Griff—and Hackett?—expect him to back them up some time in the future.

"How's your friend? Still under the weather—or is he six feet under the ground?"

"He'll live," Griff said. His arm tensed and Slocum got ready to draw.

"There you are, Mr. Slocum" came Carter Stevenson's words from the corridor. "I wondered what was keeping you. I see you've met Henry's foreman."

"Griff here is foreman of the Colorado Prince?"

"A good mine, sir," Stevenson said. "But not as good as the Little Pittsburgh, no matter what Henry claims. It's not even as good when you add in the take from the Little King Mine." Stevenson posted himself between the two men and turned to Griff. "You can tell Henry that his latest offer for the Little Pittsburgh Mining Company is still too low. He could offer me ten times as much and I wouldn't take it. That mine is my life!"

Stevenson put his arm around Slocum's shoulder and guided him into the hallway ahead of him. Slocum didn't want Stevenson catching any bullets meant for him, but he wasn't going to argue much, either, about using him as a shield. Griff would put a bullet between his shoulder blades, given the chance.

"Do come along to the track, Mr. Slocum. They're just starting the sundown races. We can bet on a race or two, then you can be off, if you need to go anywhere."

"They race at night? Isn't that dangerous?" Slocum spoke to keep Stevenson occupied. His sharp green eyes scanned the room. Linette sat with her back to him, across the table from the bulky Henry Hackett. Whatever the mine owner had said, she found it to be hilarious and was laughing uproariously.

Behind him he heard Griff moving. He kept Stevenson between him and the backshooting murderer. Only when he reached the stairs did Slocum heave a sigh of relief. The Leadville Trotting and Racing Club might be a fancy-ass place, but he could have ended up dead and buried and no one would have much cared.

Slocum glanced at Carter Stevenson. Even his benefactor wouldn't much care if it was found out he wasn't as rich as he made out. Men like this cared only for money and the power it bought them.

Even as this thought crossed his mind Slocum began to seethe. What the hell was Linette doing with Henry Hackett? What was Hackett doing to the woman?

"It's just over there. We can walk. I've been trying to get the club to put in seats on the fourth floor so we can watch from up there, but there's some trouble with the notion. I say, if Leadville can have an opera house, I see no reason why we shouldn't get decent box seats for the racetrack!"

Slocum saw large gas torches being lit around the track. He shook his head. Nighttime racing. What else did these rich, idle men do in their leisure time?

"Do the torches cause the horses to shy?" Slocum asked. He followed Stevenson to a betting window. The horses running were chalked in on a board, the odds posted beside them.

"Don't notice if they do," Stevenson said, distracted. He fumbled in his pocket and pulled out a wallet thick with greenbacks. He put down a five-hundred-dollar bet on a twenty-to-one long shot.

Slocum touched his pocket. The money he had won in Denver had dwindled steadily. Leadville was an expensive place, and he had only been there for a day. If he bet every nickel he had, he couldn't match a quarter of Stevenson's bet.

"Go on, Mr. Slocum. Place your bet. It's almost post time."

"I prefer studying the horses before a race. You obviously know them better than I do, putting down a bet like that on a long shot."

"You can't make money without risking it," Stevenson

said. He was slightly flushed with the excitement of the bet. "But do hurry, sir. The horses are ready."

At the mine owner's insistence, Slocum put down a larger bet than he would have in other circumstances. And he spread it among the three horses with the best odds. Just as he took the slip of paper with his bet on it, a bell rang and betting stopped. He and Stevenson reached the fence just as the horses blasted past them.

Slocum had seventy-five dollars riding on the outcome of the race, but he kept his eyes peeled for Griff. Winning would be nice, but getting a load of buckshot in the back was more likely if he didn't pay attention.

"There, Mr. Slocum, there! Oh . . ." Stevenson's words trailed off as his horse fell farther behind with every stride. Two of the horses crossing the finish favored Slocum. He had picked the win and show horses.

"You are the winner, Mr. Slocum. Let's see." Stevenson squinted as the tally was printed out on a large chalkboard. "You've won almost two hundred dollars."

"Not as much as if you'd won," Slocum pointed out. This caused Stevenson to brighten.

"Quite so, sir. You *are* a gentleman."

Stevenson turned back to study the horses slated for the next race. Slocum saw Griff enter the track and walk along one rail. If the man was coming for him, it was time to drift away. He could always explain to Carter Stevenson later—if he stayed alive.

Slocum slipped away from the mining mogul and melted into the thin crowd behind. He wanted to get away from Griff. And he wanted to find Linette Clayton. This time she wouldn't slip away from him. She'd have to explain what the hell was going on.

9

Slocum stood outside the mile-and-a-quarter track and waited for the next race to get under way before he slipped back to the Leadville Trotting and Racing Club. He wanted to make sure Griff had as hard a time as possible tracking him. Even if he found Stevenson, Griff wasn't stupid enough to do anything to the man now. Not with hundreds of spectators likely to see him.

Slocum's steps lengthened until he came to the side door of the impressive four-story redbrick building that housed the club. He looked around. No one saw him through the pitch darkness of the Leadville night. He tried the door and, to his surprise, found it open. It took him only a few seconds to get inside, fasten the door behind him to keep Griff from sneaking up behind him and backshooting him, then took the stairs two at a time until he reached the dining room on the fourth floor.

He had come out in still another service entrance. He peered around the door and saw the impassive maître d'hôtel presiding over the few members left in the room. Slocum tried to find Linette. She was nowhere to be seen. He con-

sidered calling a waiter over and asking after her, then forgot
the idea immediately. Henry Hackett looked to be a man
who didn't take anything for granted. He might have left a
tidy retainer for any of the staff reporting interest in the
lovely Linette.

Slocum retreated down the stairs, pausing for a moment
when he reached the second floor. He heard women's laughter. He pushed through a door and walked circumspectly
down a back hallway. Slocum quickly discovered what went
on here. This floor was given over to nothing but bedrooms.
He didn't have to be any kind of genius to know what went
on in the sumptuous rooms. Miners bought whores and a
quick tumble in a crib hardly longer than the men were tall.

The mine owners were far more genteel in their pleasures.
And the women were more refined. But they were still
whores, no matter where they laid down.

Slocum knew his rising anger wasn't justified. There
wasn't any reason to get mad at either the painted women
or the men they slept with. It just stuck in his craw that
Linette might be screwing Hackett with the mistaken notion
that she was going to find out who had killed her sister.

The sounds coming from behind a couple of the doors
was unmistakable. If Linette and Hackett were in either
room, Slocum didn't want to know. From a third room he
heard the clinking of glass touching glass. Cautiously opening the door, he peered inside.

He almost called out to Linette. She was pouring wine
from a crystal decanter into a fancy goblet. Slocum bit back
his whoop of glee at finding her when he saw she poured
not one but two glasses. That meant she wasn't alone.

He told himself he should leave Linette Clayton, leave
Leadville, leave the entire territory of Colorado—but he
couldn't. Slocum snaked his way into the dimly lit room
and hid behind deep, plush red-velvet curtains hanging be-

side the door. He was able to overhear everything said in the room.

"There's no reason for you to be like this, my dear," Hackett said in his gravelly voice.

"Like what, Mr. Hackett?" Linette was playing coy. Slocum drew back the curtain a mite and chanced a look into the room. She sat by herself in a chair, Henry Hackett perched on a low footstool in front of her. He looked like a grotesque toad, ready to send its tongue lashing out at a reckless fly coming too close.

"There's no need to resist my advances. I am a very wealthy man. I can give you anything you want—if you give me what I want." Hackett reached out a pudgy hand and stroked Linette's upper leg. She moved and cleverly avoided him when he tried to work his hand under her skirt.

"I am not without my own sources of income, sir," she said. "What we have is rare. We are good friends."

"That is nice, but I'd like us to be . . . closer," Hackett whispered in a husky voice.

Slocum held himself back. It wouldn't do if he burst in on them. Besides, his worst suspicions were unfounded. Linette was withstanding the mining magnate's advances, not succumbing to them.

"There's so much danger in the world," she said. "Look at what happened in Denver."

"You worry too much, my dear," Hackett said. "Those three men were unfortunate victims of a botched robbery attempt, nothing more. It is just coincidence that they were all officers of the Iron-Silver Mining Company."

"I've heard other officers have died recently. I don't want to think *you* are in danger. After all, you are the president of the company." Linette reached out and touched Hackett's cheek. His jowls bounced in response.

"I have guards."

"Where is Griff?" Linette sipped at her white wine.

Slocum knew she was playing a dangerous game now, and wondered if she had guessed Hackett's henchman was one of her sister's murderers. From the ease with which she spoke, he didn't think so. Linette couldn't be that good an actress in the face of the man likely to have sent Griff and the other two bushwhackers to the wedding.

"I gave him the night off. I have nothing to fear from you, do I?"

"I don't know, Mr. Hackett. Many men have described me as . . . dangerous."

"Exciting, perhaps," Hackett said with a laugh, "but dangerous? That's not possible. Only a man can be dangerous."

Linette smiled, but Slocum saw how she held back her acid retort. He wasn't going to bet that she was more deadly than Hackett, not until he knew more about the situation in Leadville. Slocum nervously shifted his weight from foot to foot, wanting the assignation between Linette and Hackett to end.

"I really must be going, Mr. Hackett," Linette said, finishing her wine in a gulp. "Thank you for such a nice dinner. We'll have to do this again."

"Again?" Hackett seemed stunned at Linette's decision for a sudden departure. "You're staying."

"No, I'm not—not tonight."

"Not tonight," Hackett said, his voice turning frosty. "When?"

Linette spun out of his grasping hands and lightly kissed him on the cheek. "Soon, Henry, soon. Good night!"

Hackett started to do more than protest her sudden farewell, but Linette was already putting her shawl around her shoulders and going out the door. Slocum grabbed her, putting his hand over her mouth. When she saw who her abductor was, she stopped struggling. Slocum pulled the door shut with a bang.

"Quiet," he whispered. "Let Hackett think you've gone." He pushed the velvet drapery to one side and watched Hackett. He wasn't sure what he expected, but Henry Hackett was obviously pissed as hell about Linette deserting him. Slocum couldn't tell but he thought he saw a bulge at the man's groin.

Linette had that effect on men. She certainly had that effect on Slocum.

Hackett heaved his vast bulk up off the stool, and grumbling, the mine owner left the posh suite of rooms, obviously irate.

He paused at the door and looked up and down the hall. Hackett bellowed something. Feet came running. He left the room and closed the door, shutting Slocum off from hearing any of what went on outside.

"His bodyguard," Linette ventured. "He probably had Griff planted at the end of the hall. He'll be puzzled when Griff reports that I didn't leave the building."

"It wasn't Griff," Slocum said, remembering how the man had come after him at the nearby race track.

"How can you be so sure?"

"Griff was one of the three who shot down Angelica at the wedding," Slocum said. He saw no reason to beat around the bush. "I killed another back in Denver. He was getting on the same stagecoach I was to come up here on. You remember the ruddy-faced man who lost at poker the night before?"

Linette nodded dully.

"That was him. Just coincidence, I think, but it's hard to tell. He might have been spying on you, since you're Angelica's sister. I winged the third man out on the road up to Carter Stevenson's mine. He and Griff tried to bushwhack Stevenson."

"I heard about that. Everyone says it was just road agents."

"They weren't out to rob him; they wanted him dead. What have you found out?" Slocum skirted the matter of Linette leaving him wounded in Denver.

"I nosed around and figured out Henry Hackett knows more about the deaths of the other officers of his company than he's letting on. I didn't realize Griff was one of the killers." Linette sounded stunned at this. "I just thought Henry might be a target, like Rupert."

"He might be behind it, but I don't know why. Just killing off other officers doesn't get him too far. The dead officers' shares of the company go to their heirs, not to Hackett."

"That might not be true," Linette said. She threw her arms around Slocum's neck and buried her face in his chest. He smelled the freshness of her hair and felt her body heaving against his. "I don't understand, but I think the shares go back to the company if the officer dies."

Slocum stopped worrying about what the hell was going on in Leadville. He had Linette in his arms again, and that was all that mattered.

"Do you think it's safe to get out of here?" he asked. "Or will Hackett keep looking for you?"

"He's a persistent man. He won't give up easily."

Slocum knew it was foolhardy staying in this posh suite, but leaving the Leadville Trotting and Racing Club building wasn't going to be easy, not with Hackett's men on the lookout for them.

"Will anyone else come to use this room?"

"It's Hackett's," she said. "At least it belongs to the Iron-Silver Mining Company, and he is the partnership's president." She looked up, her blue eyes dancing mischievously. "It seems a shame to waste such a fine bed, doesn't it, John?"

Slocum turned to look at the fancy four-poster bed in the corner of the room. It had a feather mattress on it that was so soft, Slocum worried about being pulled down into its depths and suffocating. But that wouldn't happen if he had something solid under him.

Or someone—like Linette.

He reached over and ran his fingers through her midnight-black hair. She tossed her head back, closed her eyes, and turned her ruby-red lips up for him to kiss. He did. Pulse racing wildly, he reached down and caught up the woman, carrying her to the bed. He gently placed her in the center of the bed. Slocum started unfastening the laces of her blouse when Linette let out a tiny gasp.

He stopped, rolling onto his side and reaching for his six-shooter. He thought Hackett had returned and found them.

"John, look!" Linette pointed to the canopy above them.

Slocum had to smile. A large mirror reflected every activity that went on in the bed. Slocum had to shake his head in amazement. The rich knew how to live.

"I'm glad he's gone and you're here, John," Linette said. Her fingers worked on his shirt. She spent as much time looking up into the mirror as she did staring at his broad, bare chest.

Slocum discovered the fascination when he went back to undressing Linette. The laces came free and her breasts poked just past the fabric. He turned and looked up. The view was deliciously different. He rolled back, his mouth seeking the hard, tight pennies of her breasts. The nipples trembled as he used his tongue on them. Sucking harder, he got her to moan softly.

Together they rolled over, Linette on top. Slocum stared at the woman's back in the mirror overhead. It was still chastely covered. He kept up his oral assault on her nipples as he worked to strip her naked to the waist. This gave him an even better view.

His fingers worked over her bare back, stroking, stimulating. Slocum wasn't sure if the feel of her smooth skin or the sight of his hands working against her back aroused him the most. There was no denying that he was excited.

When Linette released his tensed manhood, that, too, showed clearly in the mirror above them.

"This is delightful," she said, moving down his body like a sidewinder slithering along a sand dune. She lay on her side so she could properly attend to his hard length with her lips—and watch what she was doing in the mirror.

Slocum had to close his eyes when the sensation of her mouth on his shaft got too much to bear. He fought to keep himself under control. He wanted more, lots more, from Linette. But her tongue worked on all the right places to set him on fire inside.

His green eyes flickered open and he watched what she was doing for a moment. His passion-hard staff would vanish between her lips, then slowly reappear. Slocum had to reach down and pull Linette gently away. He wanted more than this.

More!

As she came to lie beside him, the raven-haired woman kicked free of her skirt. Slocum was treated to the sight of a completely naked body beside him. Then he was scrambling to get his trousers off.

"Silly, you're hurrying too much," she said. "Let me help."

Slocum wasn't sure how much Linette was helping as she worked his boots free, then began pulling off his trousers. The sight of all this occurring in the mirror above them added fuel to the fire starting to burn in his loins.

"I can't take any more of this," he said. "I need you *now*!"

Linette giggled as she rolled onto her back, her thighs spreading for him. Slocum had to look up just once more. The inviting patch of dark fur nestled between her legs glistened with dewy drops. Linette had gotten as enthusiastic about this as he had.

Then Slocum rolled atop her, fitting himself snugly between her legs. Linette's thighs pressed in on either side of his body. He poked a few times, then touched the core of her being.

Warmth engulfed him. He pushed himself up on his arms and levered his hips forward until he was buried balls-deep in her clinging, moistly hot center. He heard Linette gasp. Then she tightened around him like a hangman's noose fastened around his neck.

"I never thought it would be this much fun, John. I can see what you're doing! It's great!"

Her fingernails dug into his back, urging him to move. Slocum pulled out of her heated core, then paused to get his balance. The fiery tide of his come built deep in his loins. It churned and boiled and threatened to explode at any instant. Slocum wanted to make this last as long as possible.

Linette Clayton was gorgeous. Her body was perfect. And she did things to him no other woman ever had.

His hips swung forward. He speared deep into her again. They both groaned with the force of his penetration. She clawed at him as her desire mounted. Slocum forgot everything except the flames licking away at his insides. The shallow trails her nails left on his back were forgotten. The pressure building along his wounded side disappeared in his desire to possess her totally.

"John, it's so good. It . . . it's so beautiful!" Linette gasped and lifted herself up off the bed. She tried to jam her body as close to his as possible. He sank even deeper into her, something he hadn't thought possible.

The torrid rush as he spilled his seed caused them both to sob and moan in joy. Spent, they collapsed to the soft bed and lay in each other's arms.

Only then did Slocum hazard a look up at the mirror. He expected it to be steamed over. It still reflected back a true—and beautiful—picture of Linette Clayton.

"There's never been anyone like you," he said honestly. He felt slightly stunned at having said such a thing aloud. He was a drifter, a man without roots. What was he doing making such a play for any woman, much less one as lovely as Linette Clayton?

"I never *dreamed* there'd be anyone like you, John," she answered. She snuggled closer, but Slocum noticed that she positioned herself so she could watch the mirror above.

This was fine with Slocum. He had the most beautiful woman in the world next to him. Whatever kept her happy pleased him, at least for the time being.

He almost laughed aloud when he thought that they had made love in the bed Henry Hackett had reserved for himself. This was too good for the likes of the mining magnate. Too damn good by half.

10

Slocum stretched on the feather mattress and sighed in contentment. He couldn't remember when he had felt this good before.

He came fully awake when he remembered where he was. Linette lay beside him in the soft bed, her hair spread on the white-linen pillowcase like a dark halo. Slocum sat up and reached for his pistol. Something had alerted him, and he wasn't sure what it was.

Getting out of bed and silently walking to the door, he pressed his ear against its thick, cold, wooden panel. He heard nothing from the hall outside. This didn't amount to a hill of beans, though. Slocum wasn't sure he'd be able to hear anything out there, unless it was Sherman's entire Army marching through Joseph Johnston's troops on their way to Savannah.

Slocum padded across the room to a window and looked down into the Leadville street. It was just before dawn. Miners were already at their jobs, an hour into their twelve-hour shifts. That didn't explain why Griff and Henry Hackett stood below, arguing. Slocum thought he knew the topic.

Hackett wasn't pleased that his foreman had lost his prey the night before.

From the angry gestures he made, Griff wasn't too pleased with the way things were going, either. Slocum tried to pull up the window. A single quick shot would eliminate the last of the men responsible for Angelica Clayton's death. The window sash stuck. Try as he might, he couldn't get it to budge.

And it was just as well. He saw a third man joining Griff and Hackett. The man walked slowly, as if in pain. From his vantage point Slocum made out the man's face. He had seen him before—when he'd shot him down during the Carter Stevenson ambush.

Slocum cursed under his breath. He'd thought he had killed the second of the men responsible for shooting up the wedding. He had only wounded the man. The one in Denver was definitely dead. But Slocum had two more to go, not just Griff.

"John?" came Linette's sleepy call from the bed. "Where are you?"

"Quiet," he cautioned. "Come take a look at these men."

Naked, she joined him at the window. She shivered in the early-morning chill. "This had better be worth it," she said, rubbing sleep from her eyes.

"There. Do you recognize them?"

"Why, it's Henry Hackett and his foreman, Griff. The third man I don't think I've seen before."

"Griff and the other man were the ones trying to bush-whack Stevenson."

"And the ones responsible for killing Angelica?"

He felt her body tense. He gripped his Colt even tighter. He didn't want Linette grabbing it from him and opening up on the men below. At this range he might be able to take out one. Linette wouldn't stand a chance of doing more

than scaring them a mite. He didn't want to warn Griff or
the other man before he pulled the trigger. They'd shown
they were slippery sons of bitches.

And Hackett? Slocum wasn't sure where the fat mine
owner fit into this.

"I want them, John. I want them so bad, it burns my
tongue."

"They'll pay for what they did to your sister," Slocum
said.

"And to you," she said, her fingers lightly dancing over
the healing wounds on his side. Her touch was light and
cool and soothing. Slocum gave the men in the street one
last look, then turned to Linette. They kissed until he broke
it off.

"We can't stay here much longer. There's no telling when
Hackett might decide to drop in."

"It would be hard to explain our situation, wouldn't it?"
she said, a glint of mischief in her blue eyes. She ran her hands
over his naked body. "What?" she said in mock horror.
"You don't like that? Do you like this any better?"

Linette stepped back and began stroking her own sleek,
white body. Slocum took a deep breath, hoping this would
calm his racing pulse. It didn't.

"We've got to go," he said firmly. He wasn't going to be
caught buck naked by Griff or anyone.

"Be like that," Linette said almost primly. She turned and
fetched her clothing. Slocum got dressed, keeping one eye on
the woman while she slipped into her clothing. This was almost as exciting for him as what they had done the night before
under the mirrored canopy.

"What do we do now?" she asked, patting her black hair
into place.

Slocum didn't have a good answer for her. There was more
afoot in Leadville than just killing off a few officers in a min-

ing company. Hackett was probably at the putrid heart of the plot, but Slocum didn't have any proof of that. More to the point was bringing Griff and his partner to justice.

"There's no one we can depend on," Slocum said. "Whatever we do, it's all up to us."

"What about Carter Stevenson? Do you think he would help?"

"I don't want to get him involved," Slocum said. "This isn't his fight—not like it's ours."

"So?"

"You go back to my hotel and stay there."

"But my things are at—"

"It doesn't matter where they are. Griff will be waiting for you to return. Don't let him get to you."

"You think he'd kidnap me?"

Slocum didn't answer that. He knew the man was as likely to kill Linette as he was to kidnap her. There wasn't money on the line in a kidnapping, though. Griff would use the lovely woman as a lever to get to Slocum. He wasn't sure if Hackett had tied the two of them together, but Slocum wasn't going to chance it.

Linette had to be kept out of the line of fire. Such thinking worried Slocum. He usually figured a person ought to follow their own instincts, and here he was trying to do what he thought was right for Linette. He knew she'd be back with Hackett, pumping him for information if he didn't stop her.

"I won't just sit around, John."

"You won't be," he said, thinking hard. "Try to piece as much of this together as you can. I need to know what Hackett is up to—if he's the one behind it all."

"He must be!" she exclaimed. "Griff is his foreman. You said Griff and the other fellow were the ones who killed Angelica."

"We've got to be certain," he said. "Now, do as I say. I'll be by the hotel later to see how you're doing."

She glared at him. He tried to think of something better to say to keep her off the Leadville streets. Nothing came to him. He knew the task he had given her was trivial—and so did she.

They left the suite and found the back stairs. Slocum worried that Griff might be patrolling outside the building, but they managed to get away without being seen. Slocum and Linette went to his hotel room. He changed from his ragged clothing into more durable trail gear. She sat and watched in dour silence. He doubted she would stay there very long after he left, but he hoped she would. He had a few people to check on before rejoining her.

Their parting was somewhat strained, Linette not happy at being left out.

"It'll be all right," he told her. "I've got people to see, then I'll be back. You won't leave, will you?"

"Reckon not," she said. "Just don't take too long. I'm missing you already, and you haven't even left yet!"

He kissed her, then forced himself to hurry off. Slocum hardly trusted himself any longer. It would be too easy to stay with Linette. In the long run that wouldn't satisfy either of their desires for revenge on Griff and his partner.

Slocum stopped for a moment in front of the Pioneer Club Saloon. He touched the golden medallion in his pocket that would gain him entry. He frowned as he remembered how he had obtained the membership token. Just bringing the preacher to the manager's attention had warranted the membership.

Slocum had wondered about it at the time, but other matters had intruded. He had a better handle on them now. His curiosity was getting the better of him. But should he go into the saloon and do some careful questioning, or would he be better off finding the preacher man and just watching?

The decision came quickly. He saw the preacher leaving the side door of the Pioneer Club Saloon. Following the man was easy enough since the parson made no attempt to throw off anyone tracking him.

The preacher walked briskly down Chestnut Street, then turned and went into the miners' shacks, running along streets dead-ending onto Chestnut. From time to time he glanced at a small piece of paper in his hand. When he came to one tumbled-down shack, he stopped, double-checked the sheet, then knocked on the door.

Slocum thought the hinges would come undone, the preacher knocked so hard. A few seconds later a grizzled man came to the door. The preacher talked quietly with him for several minutes, then reached into his pocket and passed over an envelope.

The man in the shack took it, pulling out a slip of paper from the envelope. He scratched his shaggy head, then nodded and waved the preacher away.

Slocum waited until the clergyman was gone before going to the shack. He peered between the cracks in the wall. Inside, the man hunkered forward over a table, the slip of paper in front of him. What interested Slocum the most was the small stack of greenbacks beside the note. The preacher had paid the miner for something—but what?

The man growled, stuffed both money and note into his coat pocket, and left. Slocum ducked out of sight. He thought he knew where the man was going with his windfall. He was right. The miner hightailed it for the nearest saloon.

Slocum let him get situated inside before entering. He took a deep breath as he looked around. At this time of day most miners were several hundred feet underground, toiling at blasting and digging the precious metals locked in stone.

Slocum went to the bar and dropped a piece of the scrip he carried onto it. ''Drinks for everybody in the house,'' he said loud enough to be overheard by the miner at the table in the rear. "This is my lucky day. I won at the races last night."

"Congratulations," the barkeep said, taking the greenback and replacing it with a shot of trade whiskey. He looked around, then smirked. "There's just about enough folks in here to chew up that twenty."

"That's fine. They're all my friends," Slocum said. He knocked back the whiskey and wondered if the miner would take the bait.

He did.

When he finished both the drink he'd ordered and the one Slocum had bought, he motioned Slocum over to his table.

"I had a run of luck myself. Came into some money. Let me buy you a drink to pay you back."

"Luck feeds luck," Slocum said, pulling up a chair. "That's mighty kind of you."

"Been out of work for a month," the miner said. "Strained my back something fierce."

"Then you got a job?" Slocum prodded.

"Just as good. Maybe better." He wasn't going to say anything more—right now. Slocum finished the drink, then ordered a bottle. That exhausted his store of twenties. He'd have to move down to the ten-dollar greenbacks if he had to buy much more.

"There's nothing like having money in your pocket," Slocum said. He and the miner drank for a few more minutes, the miner putting away two for every one Slocum drank.

Tipsy, the miner began letting more and more slip about the source of his money.

"A preacher? I can't believe it. I thought they only asked for money. You mean, this one *gave* you money?"

"Not gave. He found work for me. I got to find a gent and . . ." The miner's voice trailed off.

''What do you have to do for the money? I can use some ex-tra money,'' Slocum said. ''Not that I'd want to muscle in on your territory.''

''I don't know exactly what I got to do for it,'' the miner said. He fumbled in his pocket and pulled out the slip of paper. ''My eyes ain't so good. Too much time in the mines, you know.'' He held the paper so that Slocum knew that the prob-lem was being unable to read, not see.

''Let me give that a looking over.'' Slocum nodded as he worked through the two lines of instructions on the note. It was about as he expected. The preacher was recruiting strong-arm help. He'd drift around and find the miners who wouldn't ask too many questions about how they made their money.

All the note gave was a time and a place. But Slocum knew what it meant. Someone was supposed to die.

''Wish I could get a job like this,'' Slocum said, handing the note back.

''Yeah?''

''Imagine,'' Slocum went on, pretending that the miner knew what the note said. ''All you have to do is wait for the preacher to come back and tell you what he wants. You know what they call this? A retainer. You're getting paid for not doing a damn thing but wait back at your house.''

''I am?''

''Surely do envy you.'' Slocum heaved himself to his feet. ''Me, I got to get to work.''

''Thanks for the drinks, mister.''

Slocum touched the rim of his Stetson, then quickly left the saloon. He had a rendezvous to keep for the man. It took longer than he thought to find the Ace in the Hole Casino. Slo-cum checked his watch and saw he didn't have much time. The preacher had been getting a band of men together for some skullduggery, and it was almost time for them to start for their target.

He circled the wood-frame building but didn't see the

preacher or anyone else he recognized. Slocum frowned. He could read. He hadn't misinterpreted the note the miner had been given.

The back of the casino was deserted. Action inside was slow, since most of Leadville was hard at work in the mines. The gambling wouldn't start in earnest until the end of the first shift after sundown. Slocum looked inside but didn't see anything that drew his attention.

He went back onto the boardwalk in front of the casino and looked up and down the dusty street. The sun was beginning to burn the town. Slocum found a rickety chair and pulled it up. He rocked back and hooked his legs around the front chair legs. Tipping his hat down over his eyes, he decided he ought to wait and see what happened.

When it came, it came fast.

He heard the thunder of horses' hooves in the street. He moved his hat back on his head and tried to make out the riders in the cloud of dust. They were almost even with him in the street when he saw Griff swinging the scattergun around.

Slocum moved with blinding speed, and it almost wasn't fast enough.

The double-barreled sawed-off shotgun erupted and cut through the wall he had been leaning against. He felt the heavy buckshot take off his hat. He hit the rough planks of the walk and rolled. A second rider opened up on him.

By the time Slocum got his Colt Navy out, the owl hoots had turned a corner and were pounding off in the direction of the mountains. Slocum stared at the pistol in his hand, then angrily jammed it back into his cross-draw holster.

He had been set up and had almost died.

If he hadn't had a score to settle before, he did now. And he knew just the place to start. He went off in search of the conniving preacher man.

11

Slocum stopped outside the Pioneer Club Saloon and gave it a once-over. He didn't expect to see the preacher man back there—not yet, anyway. The preacher wouldn't get paid until Griff reported back that his bushwhacking plan had worked.

Slocum wondered if Conrad, the manager of the Pioneer Club Saloon, was behind all the killing. He doubted it. Henry Hackett looked like too good a choice. With the huge stream of money flowing from the silver mines around Leadville, anyone could be bought. Slocum smiled crookedly as he stared at the posh gambling club. He pulled out the gold medallion that would gain him entry, then began flipping it in the air, watching it sparkle as it spun.

Who owned the Pioneer Club Saloon? He had no idea. Conrad might work directly for Hackett. It certainly made sense. Conrad had set the trap, using the preacher to plant the bait. Then Hackett's foreman finished the job with his shotgun.

It all fell together in Slocum's head. There might be a few twists he had missed, but he didn't think so. Working backward from the preacher seemed to be his best bet. He wanted to be sure everyone in the chain got what was coming to him.

He slid the medallion back into his vest pocket when he saw the parson stalking along, head down against the cold wind blowing down Chestnut Street. The preacher passed within a dozen feet of Slocum without seeing him.

Slocum trailed the preacher into the club, flashing his medallion as he passed the bouncer stationed at the door. Slocum gauged the huge man's reaction carefully. Not a flicker of interest crossed the man-mountain's face. Whoever had ordered Slocum's death hadn't bothered telling the hired help about it.

The preacher made a beeline straight for the club's manager. The manager looked up when the parson came up. Conrad gestured to the bouncer to keep away. Then he and the minister huddled together. Conrad shook his head several times, the last time emphatically enough for Slocum to know that they argued. The preacher shoved his hand out, as if demanding money.

Slocum edged closer, ordering a whiskey at the bar. Turning a bit, he overheard the conversation.

"I want my money for the chore. I did as you wanted," complained the preacher.

"I haven't heard back."

"I don't know what this is all about, Mr. Conrad. I found a down-on-his-luck miner like you told me and gave him the sealed note and the greenbacks. What else is there for me to do?"

"There's more," said Conrad.

Slocum sipped at his whiskey, thinking hard. The preacher looked to be an innocent dupe caught up in Conrad's scheme. He was glad he hadn't accosted the preacher directly. The minister had no idea he was setting a man up to be ambushed and killed.

"When can I expect my share of the money?"

"You could have held back some," Conrad said. "You didn't have to give it all to the miner."

"I don't understand. Why not? I thought you were being generous with your charity."

"Charity?" Conrad laughed harshly. "Sure, charity. Hell, it's probably all right. Here." The club manager fumbled in his wallet and pulled out a sheaf of greenbacks. He counted quickly and passed a few to the preacher.

"Thank you for your Christian kindness, both to the church's building fund and to the indigent of this sin-racked city. If you need any more errands run, let me know."

"You'll be the first to know if I need more help," Conrad said, a nasty smirk on his face.

The preacher left, his stride long and confident. He had helped the needy and gained much-needed money for his building fund. How was he to know he had been a cat's-paw? Using the preacher this way made Slocum even angrier.

Conrad was involved with Griff and Hackett. Linette thought she knew what was going on, but Slocum wasn't so sure. Wheels turned within wheels. Angelica Clayton's death was only a small part of whatever went on in Leadville.

Slocum finished his whiskey and hunched over the bar as Conrad pushed behind him. The man didn't even notice him. Slocum strained and heard what the club manager already had. Horses' hooves pounded hard outside. It had to be Griff and his accomplice, returning to report on their murderous attempt on his life.

Conrad vanished into the back of the saloon. Slocum started after him but quickly saw that the bouncer would stop him before he reached the back offices. Instead Slocum started up the stairs to the second floor. Once there, he crossed the large, almost deserted gambling room and found a back window. He pried it open, not caring that the four men in the room were staring at him curiously.

From this second-story vantage he had a good view of everything being done below. Slocum saw two horses, all lathered from a hard run, tethered to the back porch railing. He couldn't see the riders, but he didn't have to. Their loud voices drifted up to him.

". . . Griff, here, says we hit him. I say that's a crock of shit. He was rolling around on the boardwalk when we turned the corner. We missed the son of a bitch!"

"Harrison's still all shook up from his gunshot," Griff said. "He isn't seeing clear. I hit him with the first load of buckshot. I finished him with the second barrel."

"You missed him," Harrison said sullenly.

Slocum smiled. Harry—Harrison—had to be the one he had wounded during the attempt on Carter Stevenson's life. All the players in this deadly drama were assembled. It was time for him to pull down the curtain on them once and for all.

He hiked his leg up and climbed over the windowsill. He heard a small murmur pass through the gamblers in the casino, but he ignored them. He got out on the slippery, wood-shingled roof and edged down. Just as Slocum was certain he could take the three, his right boot shot out from under him. Grabbing wildly, he barely kept from tumbling over the verge and to the ground.

But the noise of his fall alerted Griff and Harrison.

"What the hell's going on, Conrad?" demanded Griff.

The deadly sound of pistols cocking told Slocum he had only a few seconds before the men figured out where the noise had come from and started shooting at its cause. He wiggled onto his belly, flat on the roof. His Colt came free of its holster, and he readied himself for a gunfight.

His commanding officer during the war had always said the high ground was the place to be. Slocum cursed when he realized that the major hadn't been trapped on a roof. Bullets ripped up through the shingles, sending splinters flying all around him.

Slocum couldn't shoot back unless he had a better idea where they were below him.

"I got him" came Griff's confident voice. "I plugged the sneaky son of a bitch."

"Who is it spying on us?" asked Conrad. "Why'd anyone climb up there unless—"

Slocum tried to keep silent, but the roof began breaking under him. The bullets had cut through a support and rotted wood was giving way. He danced along, not caring if he made noise. Griff and the others would know he was untouched by their bullets soon enough.

"He's still alive!" cried Harrison. New lead came whistling through the shingles, seeking Slocum's hide. He came to the edge of the overhang, paused, then did what had to be done.

He dropped flat on his belly again, gripped the edge, and swung out. For a giddy moment the world wheeled around him. His move took the three men by surprise, though. They didn't expect him to fall into their laps like this.

Slocum didn't count on them taking long to react. He let go and dropped a dozen feet, landing hard on the ground. He hit with knees bent, and rolled. When he came to his feet, he had his six-shooter ready for action.

An incautious head poked over the railing above him on the porch. He fired and took off Harrison's hat.

"He kilt me!" the man yelled.

"You're just scratched," muttered Conrad.

Slocum duck-walked to the side of the Pioneer Club Saloon and waited for Griff to see what was happening. All Slocum needed was a hint of a head and Griff was a dead man. Slocum cursed his bad luck when Griff didn't show himself. The bushwhacker had turned suddenly cagey. Slocum knew he wasn't going to be able to hold off Griff, Harrison, and Conrad—especially when the club's manager started yelling for his brawny bouncers to help.

A window into a shallow cellar called to Slocum as a way out of his predicament. It resisted him for a moment, then came loose with a loud grating sound. Slocum dived headfirst into the basement, scraping himself as he went. He got to his feet and closed the window. Through the dirty pane of glass he saw boots moving back and forth. A quick count showed at least five men outside on his trail.

Slocum knew he had to make the best of his momentary freedom. He started for the stairs leading up into the saloon. Pausing at the top, six-shooter ready, he opened the door slowly. In the lobby stood one bouncer, arms crossed and looking pissed.

There was good reason for it. Conrad would have raised all kinds of hell about letting Slocum inside. Dead men weren't valued customers at the Pioneer Club Saloon.

Slocum slipped out quietly. The bouncer was too intent on the commotion out on the front steps to notice Slocum. Several escape routes suggested themselves to Slocum, but he wasn't looking to hightail it out of the club. He was more interested in putting a few holes in Griff and Harrison.

On silent feet, he went back up the stairs to the casino on the second floor. The gamblers again looked up from their game, puzzled at the disturbance. Slocum held his Colt down at his side so they wouldn't see it and get spooked. He went back to the window where he had crept outside before.

"Hey, mister, what's going on down in the street?" called one player. The gambler held his cards close to his chest to keep the others in the game from seeing what he held. It could have been the Second Coming and he would have played out the hand. Slocum read it in the man's cold eyes.

He wondered if the others in the poker game knew who was likely to win the large pot.

"Can't tell. Better go check," Slocum said. Again he climbed through the window. Conrad and the others would never look for him up here, not after they thought he'd hit the ground running.

Slocum walked out on the shot-up roof and waited. It didn't take long for his chance to come. Conrad and two of his bouncers came around the side of the building. The guards carried long oak ax handles. The only one carrying a pistol was the club manager.

Sunlight caught on Slocum's pistol and reflected down to warn Conrad. The man swung his pistol up. He never got the chance to fire. Slocum's aim was deadly. The shot from his ebony-handled Colt Navy caught Conrad just above the heart.

Conrad dropped without uttering a word.

The two men with Conrad took a second to realize what had happened. When they did, they let out a loud cater-wauling that could be heard halfway across Leadville. Slocum had no quarrel with them; he wasn't going to shoot down unarmed men, even if they would cave in his head, given the chance.

He made his way along the rickety roof, keeping out of sight of the men below. Slocum hesitated, wondering what had become of Harrison and Griff. Then he decided he could hunt them down later. Getting away from the Pioneer Club Saloon with his own hide in one piece was more important than revenge.

Conrad was dead, and Conrad had been the one who had set the killers on him. The preacher seemed innocent. But this didn't convince Slocum that he had gotten to the heart of the plot—or found who was the brains behind the operation. Someone had ordered Angelica Clayton's wedding shot up, and Slocum didn't think it was the dead club manager.

Slocum crawled back into the casino. Two more gamblers sat in on the poker game. The ones who had seen Slocum's earlier comings and goings whispered to the newcomers. Slocum tipped his hat politely and walked quickly to the far side of the room. He heaved open the balky corner window and saw the drainpipe within easy reach. Swinging out, he made his way to the ground.

Once more he outguessed his pursuers. The two bouncers with Conrad were shouting that their boss's murderer was in the casino. By the time everyone converged on the room, Slocum was long gone.

Halfway down the arid street, he turned and looked back at the fancy club. He reached into his pocket and pulled out the gold medallion Conrad had given him.

"Useless," he muttered. Slocum flipped it into the air and put a slug through the center as it turned in midair. The medallion went spinning off at a crazy angle, catching the rays of sunlight and sending them back to earth in crazy patterns.

"Nice shooting," observed an old man leaning against a rail by a cobbler's store.

"Just practicing," Slocum said.

"Reckon I can figure out what you're practicin' for," the old man said. He spat accurately, hitting a large black bug crawling along the boardwalk. "Two hombres left the saloon down there about five minutes ago, actin' as if someone'd set fire to their tails."

"You know them?" asked Slocum.

" 'Course I do. Who doesn't know Henry Hackett's foreman and his right-hand man? Griff and that no-account Harrison probably went to get liquored up."

"Where?"

"So you *are* after them." The old man spat again, this

time into the dusty street. ''Good. They deserve ending up like that.'' He pointed in the direction of the gold medallion.

Slocum reloaded his six-shooter while the old man put another pinch of chew between his cheek and gums. The old man's watery blue eyes never left Slocum.

''Yep, you're good enough to rid us of Griff.''

''Where?'' Slocum repeated.

''Try the Big Colorado Saloon. Don't rightly know, but I reckon Hackett owns it. Leastwise, Griff and Harrison always drink there, and nobody's ever seen 'em pay.''

Slocum started down the street, saw the plugged medallion in the dust, and picked it up. He held it up to the light. The hole was neatly bored, dead center, through the medallion. He turned and flipped it to the old man, who deftly caught it. ''Here's something to remember Griff by,'' he said.

Hackett's mine foreman wasn't going to get away with murder this time.

12

Slocum paused outside the imposing Big Colorado Saloon. There was a steady stream of miners going into the huge brick-front building. The line may have looked like thirsty ants, but Slocum saw the miners in a different light.

A sign outside the saloon promised half-price drinks for anyone working for the Iron-Silver Mining Company. The men inside would not only know one another but also they'd likely stick up for their foreman. Plucking Griff and his cohort, Harrison, from the middle of so many friends and coworkers didn't look too promising.

But Slocum wasn't going to quit now. The two men owed him. Plenty.

He peered in a dirty window and tried to find either Griff or Harrison. Neither man was to be seen. Whores worked their way through the crowd, cajoling, soliciting, making wild promises. The drinks might have been cheap, but Slocum guessed the women weren't. Henry Hackett wasn't losing a plugged nickel at the Big Colorado Saloon.

"Do something for you, fella?" came a gravelly voice. Slocum turned, reaching for his six-shooter. The woman in

113

the saloon's doorway looked as if she'd been rode hard and put away wet. She licked her rouged lips and patted at dirty strands of mousy brown hair. The lewd wink of the coal-dust-darkened eye was supposed to entice Slocum. It almost turned his stomach.

How different this woman was from Linette Clayton.

"I'm looking for the mine foreman. Griff's his name, I think. I just blew into Leadville, and a friend told me I might be able to get a job out at the Colorado Prince, or maybe the Little King."

"You don't look like a hard-rock miner to me," she said. "But I still like what I see. Come on in and have a drink. Then we can see about Griff."

"Don't have any money," Slocum lied. "That's why it's real important for me to find Griff."

She snorted in disgust. "Come on in. That mangy cayuse of a mine foreman is around somewhere. Probably with that red-haired floozy of his."

"He's got a steady woman?"

"She likes to think she is," the whore said. She turned and vanished into the bustle inside the Big Colorado Saloon. Slocum followed, hesitant about walking into a trap. Back to the wall just inside the door, he looked around. The miners he saw were too intent on drinking even to notice a newcomer in their midst. They might pay no never mind to him, but he was still on guard. Griff and Harrison knew he was alive—and they might even know he'd taken care of Conrad. If they did, that would make them even more skittish.

Slocum edged to the bar.

"Give my friend here a special," the whore said, winking broadly. Slocum saw the barkeep nod slightly to acknowledge the woman's thinly veiled request. Whatever they were giving him wasn't going to set well with him. He watched carefully but didn't see the barkeep put anything into the liquor. That didn't matter much. The entire bottle might be laced with knockout drops. The strong, cheap whiskey would cover the taste of anything less potent than a dead skunk.

"Go on," she urged. "Drink up. It's on the house. A get-acquainted drink for a new worker in the mine."

Slocum's hand remained clutched around the oversize shot glass. Thick, oily film formed on the top of the amber-colored bourbon, warning him that the barkeep was only waiting for him to drink it before slitting his throat.

"This is real kind of you. I hate to take charity. I really want to pay my own way. Where's Griff—"

The woman tensed as she looked past Slocum into the filthy mirror hanging behind the bar. Slocum turned, flinging the doctored liquor into Griff's eyes.

Slocum didn't stop there. He was too close to the mine foreman to get his six-shooter free. He reached out and caught the blinded man's right wrist and tightened his fingers around it to keep Griff from getting his own pistol out.

The whore started shouting at the top of her lungs. Slocum wasn't sure what she wanted or who the shrieks were directed at. He had himself a handful with Griff.

"You're a dead man," grunted the mine foreman. He fought to get his hand out of Slocum's steely grip.

Slocum didn't bother answering. Griff only sought to distract him. Slocum brought his left fist around in a hay-maker that caught the foreman high on the cheek, snapping his head back. Griff stepped away. When he did, Slocum followed, his knee coming up to crush anything he found in Griff's groin.

The air left the struggling miner. He gasped and doubled over. Slocum got his balance back and kicked straight for the man's face. He missed when the whore shoved him hard from behind.

He turned to her. Her face turned white under the paint she had applied to it.

"Don't kill me, mister. He . . . he's my boss."

"He's more'n that" came an amused comment from a miner watching the fight.

Slocum had no reason to go after the woman. Her fright caused her to turn and try to flee. She crashed into a solid wall of miners. Any fight inside the walls of the Big Colorado Saloon was reason for cheering and betting.

"Five on the little fella," one miner called out. A dozen others shouted their bets. It took Slocum a second to realize that the man had meant him. He stood six feet and carried the whipcord strength of a cowboy used to working the range. Next to Griff—next to any of the hugely muscled hard-rock miners—he was "the little fella."

Slocum swung around, fist ready to land again on Griff's head. He missed by a mile. Griff had collapsed to the sawdust-covered floor and was writhing in pain. Slocum did connect with another miner pushing to the front of the crowd. The blow bounced off his chest. Slocum got the impression that if the miner hadn't been paying attention, he wouldn't even have noticed the impact.

As it was, he grunted and turned a stormy face to Slocum.

"You shouldna done that."

Slocum's strength was fading fast. He had not fully recovered from the shotgun blast suffered at Angelica's wedding. To fight this mountain of a man was out of the question.

Ducking, Slocum avoided the first clumsy punch from the miner. The man didn't know how to fight, but Slocum saw he had the stamina and the hard muscle to keep flailing away for hours. If he hadn't hit anything by then—and killed it with a single blow—he'd probably give up and go drink some more. Slocum wasn't up to the dodging and dipping it would take to get free.

Slocum dropped to the floor and kicked out. The sole of one foot caught the miner on the kneecap. Slocum hooked his other foot behind the man's heel. Like a tree being cut down, the miner toppled backward and crashed to the floor.

Slocum rolled and got to his feet and his hand went to his six-shooter. If nothing else, he'd get rid of Griff once and for all. To his chagrin, the mine foreman was nowhere to be seen.

"Where'd Griff go?" he demanded of the barkeep.

"Harrison—" The barkeep pointed toward the rear of the saloon. Slocum couldn't get through the heavy crowd of miners fast enough. He turned and dived headlong through the dirty window next to the door. Glass cut at his hands and face as he blasted through. He landed hard on his belly, the wind almost gone from his tortured, straining lungs. Gasping for breath, he got to his feet and stumbled to the side of the Big Colorado Saloon. To stay meant fighting more of the miners—and that meant his death.

He wanted Griff and Harrison. Then he might think about taking on the rest of Leadville.

He heard horses out behind the saloon. Stumbling rather than running, he made his way around. Inside the building he heard a full-scale donnybrook in progress. The miners didn't much care who they fought. It was all in good fun for them, a way to let off steam from their grueling twelve-hour shifts five hundred feet underground.

Slocum cocked his Colt as he rounded the building. Two men were already mounted. He lifted his pistol and fired in a smooth motion. One jerked back in the saddle, almost falling. Then both horses took off, the riders barely keeping their mount.

Slocum got off a second shot. He cursed when he missed by a country mile. He had put another slug into Harrison but had not killed the man. He seemed to have nine lives, like a cat. And Griff had been slumped forward, still hurting from the punishment Slocum had given him inside the saloon.

Slocum turned in disgust and hurried off. He had to find the livery and do something about getting a horse. He had "borrowed" the swaybacked nag before, but it wouldn't be able to keep up with the swift horses Griff and Harrison rode. He knew that if he didn't track them to ground now, he would lose them.

Putting enough of a scare into men like that caused them to hightail it for parts unknown. It wouldn't matter what Henry Hackett was paying them. Their hides were more precious than any gold the mine owner could offer them to stick around Leadville.

It took the better part of a half hour for Slocum to get a horse adequate for his needs and to saddle up to follow the fleeing pair out of Leadville. He had damn little money left, but he thought the money was well spent. The horse was a gelding, lively and well fed. He sucked up some of its energy as he rode, growing stronger the farther he got from town. It felt good to be on the trail again, away from the crush of the boomtown and its forty thousand residents.

Keen green eyes scanned the road, but he saw little trace of the fleeing men. He began to worry that he had taken the wrong road out of town and wasn't anywhere close to Griff and Harrison. Slocum slowed and finally dropped to the hard ground to study the road for some indication of where the two had gone. He walked for more than a hundred yards before he found shiny nicks in a rock in the road. He studied it and decided it was recent—not more than a few hours old. Wind and dust and rain would have rounded the sharp edges of the scratch if it had been there any longer.

He looked up and saw a fallen sign that showed a back way into the Little Pittsburgh Mining Company property. Griff and Harrison had headed for the spot where they knew they could count on finding allies. Slocum cursed loudly.

He wanted to take them out by themselves, without involving scores of others.

Their friends might not be any less guilty of murder than Griff and Harrison, but Slocum had to start somewhere. He *knew* the two men had shot up the wedding—and him. And he had seen them when they'd bushwhacked Carter Stevenson.

They were as guilty as sin, and they'd pay.

He climbed back into the saddle and put his heels to the gelding's flanks. The animal responded strongly, glad for the chance to run. In less than twenty minutes they were in the foothills. Abandoned mine shafts dotted the terrain, tailings dribbling out of the gaping mouths like stony tongues. Slocum slowed when the road gave out, and he found himself making his way across uncharted country.

Sometimes the mines came too close to the surface and left weak spots. To blunder onto one of the flimsy areas meant a plunge into a shaft that might go straight down a hundred feet or more. Slocum found enough evidence of mining activity on the hilly land to justify his caution.

But he spent too much time watching the ground and not enough scanning the knolls for his quarry. A bullet whistled past his ear. It took long seconds for him to figure out where it had come from, then he jerked on his horse's reins to get moving for cover. By then, a second leaden bee had buzzed past his head.

Slocum had been careless, but good luck had saved him. Now it was time to rely on skill rather than chance. He dropped flat and wiggled forward on his belly to find the owl hoots shooting at him. A flash of light off something metallic gave away Griff's and Harrison's positions.

"How am I going to get up there?" he muttered to himself.

His horse let out a long, wet snort, as if saying, "It's not my problem."

Slocum retrieved his Winchester from its sheath and skirted the low hummock where he'd taken cover. It was a goodly distance to the hill from where Griff and Harrison had taken their potshots, but Slocum wasn't in any hurry. He wanted their blood so bad, he could taste it.

Knowing the distance was too great for a good shot, and not having a clear shot at either man, Slocum kept low and worked his way closer. He wasn't sure if they lost sight of him or not. He hoped so, wanting to get near enough to kill them both. What worried him the most was Griff and Harrison getting spooked and scurrying off like rats.

He didn't want to have to spend days hunting them down in these treacherous mountains. They knew the area and he didn't. He wanted to end this now.

Slocum got to the foot of the hill where he had seen the silvery flash. Working his way up the barren side would be dangerous, but he was up to it. His heart raced at the prospect of finally setting the score with Griff and Harrison. He had put enough bullets into Harrison to kill the man twice over, but still he lived.

Not this time. And Griff was soon to be buzzard bait, too.

"There he is, Griff. Get him!" came the loud cry from above. Slocum hit the ground and rolled, trying to find a boulder for cover. He expected a dozen bullets to rip him open—but none came.

He got to his knees behind a large rock and waited almost a minute before poking his head out to see what was happening.

Hell broke loose, bullets flying everywhere. He dropped flat onto his stomach, puzzling over what was wrong. It finally became apparent to him. Not a single slug ricocheted off the large rock where he had taken refuge. Whoever Griff and Harrison were firing at was some distance around the hillside.

Slocum smiled crookedly. This was better than he could

have hoped for. Let the stranger draw their fire; he'd finish off both of the damn backshooters before they knew what hit them.

He chanced a quick look, then got his feet under him and dashed up the hill. He tensed as he got near the summit, expecting a trap. He forced such thoughts from his mind. Griff wasn't the type to get too cagey about these things. He was more of a walk-up-and-shoot-in-the-back sort of killer. Slocum hit the ground, his rifle ready.

Gunfire from farther down the other side of the hill told him that Harrison and Griff were still occupied with the stranger who had foolishly blundered into this deadly snare. Slocum rose to his knees and saw small movements. He had an easy shot. He lifted the Winchester to his shoulder and sighted on Griff's broad shoulders. His finger tightened slowly for the kill.

And he relaxed his trigger finger at the last instant. Griff had ducked back down, ruining a good shot. Slocum wasn't going to give himself away when victory was so close.

Swearing a blue streak, he got to his feet and moved along the ridge. No one noticed him as he moved. He found a new vantage point where Griff's back was exposed.

Something made the mine foreman turn and look back over his shoulder. For a fleeting second Slocum's cold green eyes locked with Griff's pale blue ones.

"Die, you son of a bitch!" Griff shouted, turning and firing his six-shooter wildly. Slocum didn't think the man could hit the broad side of a barn at this range with a handgun, but he reacted rather than thought. He skidded belly-down on the rocky ground to avoid the lead whining all around him. He came to rest in a prone position and caught sight of Griff's arm. He fired quickly, more interested in keeping Griff occupied than killing him now.

Slocum's Winchester came up empty. He hadn't been counting his rounds, and this irritated him. He had been too caught up in the fight to notice the details his life depended on. He rolled onto his back and found the spare cartridges in his shirt pocket, where he'd put them earlier. He loaded quickly, then kept rolling until he came to a spot where he could see downhill.

Griff wasn't in sight, but this didn't worry Slocum. The mine foreman had to be out there somewhere. Slocum had won more than his fair share of battles for the Confederacy through patience. He knew how to lay a trap, then sit and wait for it to be sprung.

"He'll get antsy," Slocum muttered to himself, his finger resting lightly on the rifle's trigger.

Five minutes passed. No shots were fired. Those five minutes dragged into ten. Slocum wasn't sure if Griff and Harrison had killed the stranger or if the man had beaten a hasty retreat. Whoever it was, it wasn't his fight.

Sudden movement caused his heart to race.

Slocum tried not to gloat. His patience had paid off. The other man had broken cover first. Griff fidgeted and moved around nervously, betraying his position. Slocum lowered the Winchester and waited for the next obvious move on the man's part. Curiosity was burning him up inside. Griff would poke his head up to see what had happened to Slocum. When he did, he'd get it blown off.

Griff's tall-crowned hat rose from behind the rock, then dropped back down a mite. Slocum wasn't going to shoot when this might be a trick. Then he saw that Griff wasn't even that subtle. He still wore his battered gray hat and now was straightening to take a gander at where his adversary hid.

Slocum had a good shot at Griff's large torso. He let out his breath as he pulled back on the trigger. The rifle exploded in his hands, cartwheeling away. This so startled Slocum, it took him several frenzied heartbeats to realize what had happened.

When he did, he was too busy trying to stay alive to worry about either his rifle or Griff.

Harrison had circled while he waited and came up on him from along the ridge. The man's ugly, triumphant laughter rolled on the cold mountain air. He held a ponderous .69 Sharps pointed squarely at Slocum's head.

Slocum was caught. There wasn't anywhere he could run or go to avoid Harrison's killing bullet.

The deadly shot sounded like thunder in the stillness.

13

The shot caused Slocum's ears to ring. But there wasn't the burning pain that went with a slug tearing a path through his dying body. He blinked and stared at Harrison. The man hadn't fired the huge buffalo rifle he held in his hands. He stood, staring stupidly. Slocum's hand flashed to his Colt Navy, then paused.

Harrison's eyes glazed, then he toppled forward and lay unmoving on the ground.

Slocum drew his six-shooter and looked in Griff's direction. He didn't see the man or his tall gray hat. Slocum checked his own body, making sure he hadn't been shot. There wasn't any reason for Harrison to have hesitated when he sighted in on Slocum.

Puzzled at the turn of events but pleased that he was still alive to be curious, Slocum went to Harrison's side. The man was already drawing flies. A large hole oozed blood in the center of his neck where the bullet had shattered his spine.

Slocum looked in the direction from which the shot must have come. He saw no one. The stranger Harrison and Griff had ambushed must have taken a measure of revenge. Slocum couldn't have been happier that it had happened when it did.

He was still alive and even more anxious to put an end to Griff's miserable life.

He looked around for the enigmatic stranger who had saved his life. After plugging Harrison in the back, the gunman had left. Slocum vowed to track him down later to thank him. Right now, though, he had business with the Colorado Prince mine foreman.

Slocum cut back and forth down the hill, keeping himself covered. He had been so startled when Harrison's first round had knocked the rifle from his hands that he'd lost sight of Griff. Without checking his watch, he doubted more than three minutes had passed from sighting on Griff's chest and being sure Harrison was dead.

"Five minutes, tops," Slocum muttered to himself. He knew the miner couldn't have gone too far. There hadn't been the pounding of horses' hooves, signaling a quick retreat on Griff's part.

Slocum spun around the rock, six-shooter cocked and ready. Nothing. He went to the spot where Griff had crouched. He studied the gravel. The rocky ground wasn't going to make tracking easy, but Slocum wasn't going to give up. He'd come too close to death for that.

He worked his way downhill, knowing that Griff hadn't gotten past him earlier. Although the mine foreman might have worked his way around the hillside, Slocum decided the best escape route would be straight down the hill.

And he was right. He saw Griff's discarded hat on the ground near the mouth of a mine shaft. Approaching slowly, he strained to hear any movement inside the mine. Not even the squeaking of rats reached his ears. Slocum put his back to the wall of the shaft, then looked around outside the mine.

The stranger who had gunned down Harrison might not know Slocum was after the bushwhacker in the pit. The hillside was deserted. A low, mournful wind howled through the rugged brush, and some dust kicked up. Other than this, Slocum saw no movement.

He spun and went into a crouch, muzzle swinging to and fro if Griff showed himself. All Slocum saw was the daunting blackness of the mine, open like a huge mouth waiting to swallow him.

He let out a low curse. To follow Griff into the shaft was to invite disaster. Slocum didn't know this mine, and Griff probably knew it like the back of his own hand. This entire area probably belonged to the Iron-Silver Mining Company and had been worked extensively. Open stopes, drifts where an ambush would come easy, cave-ins, gas—the dangers stacked the deck against Slocum.

He wasn't even sure Griff had gone into the mine. The back-shooting son of a bitch might have dropped his hat to decoy Slocum inside. A few kicks on the shaky support timbers would bring the roof crashing down to bury anyone fool enough to enter.

Slocum argued with himself about going after Griff—if the miner had even gone inside. The arguments against risking his neck in the mine outweighed waiting for Griff elsewhere. Slocum wasn't going to die underground if he could help it.

Slamming his six-shooter back into his holster, he trudged back up the hill to where Harrison had been killed. A buzzard had made a preliminary swoop down to pluck at the corpse. Ants covered the body and other insects began their gory meal. By nightfall the coyotes or wolves would have finished off the flesh.

Slocum didn't even look back as he went to find his horse. Harrison didn't deserve a proper burial.

• • •

He rode slowly back into Leadville. The town seemed no different. The miners roared and shouted drunkenly. The casinos burst at the seams with men looking to get rich quick and escape the backbreaking labor in the mines. And painted women leaned out of second-story windows to call to the men in the streets.

It wasn't any different—but it looked that way to Slocum. He had grown suddenly weary of civilization, such as it was. He wanted to leave Leadville and people behind, find himself a place under the stars a hundred miles from the nearest human. After all the killing, he wanted solitude.

He knew he wasn't likely to find it anytime soon. And as he rode down Chestnut Street memories of Linette returned to drive away the depression. She was the reason he had come to this mining town. And avenging her sister's death had been done.

Almost. Griff remained. Harrison and the other man back in Denver had paid for their treachery. Were two deaths enough?

Slocum's thoughts kept returning to Hackett's foreman. Griff had to die. Then he could feel free of the burden of revenge. He rubbed his side and felt only tenderness. He was damn near healed. The entire killing spree could come to an end.

Dismounting in front of the hotel where he'd left Linette, Slocum tied his horse to a hitching post. He went up on the boardwalk and found an iron boot scraper shaped like a boar and got the caked mud off his boots. He heaved a sigh as he walked into the hotel. Slocum wasn't sure he could talk Linette into dropping the entire matter and riding out of Leadville with him.

He was halfway up the stairs, still trying to figure out what he was going to say to her, when she came rushing down. She threw herself into his arms, almost knocking him back down the stairs. Arms circling her slender waist, he swung her around, more to keep his balance than anything else.

"You're back! John, I've been going crazy with worry. Don't leave me again. Please don't!"

He kissed her, aware that the hotel clerk stared at them. Conscious of others in the hotel lobby turning in their direction, Slocum put Linette down on the stairs.

"Come on up to the room," he said. "I've got some things to tell you." He wondered if she would agree to leave Leadville if he finished off Griff.

Seeing her again made his heart rise into his throat. He began thinking it might not be such a bad thing to let Griff be and just leave town.

"I've got so much to tell you, too, John," Linette gushed. She clung to his arm as they went to the top of the stairs. She had to stop and kiss him again before they entered his room.

"Wait," she said, cutting him off. "Hear me out. This is too good to keep."

She seated herself on the dirty bed, primly spreading her skirts around her as if preparing for a church social.

"You didn't stay put, did you?" He dropped his cross-draw holster on the low stand next to the bed, then kicked off his boots and sank beside her, tired to the bone. Slocum was afraid of what the raven-haired woman would say.

"I couldn't," she said, her cheeks flushed. "Don't think harshly of me for not obeying. This is too important." She took a deep breath. Slocum appreciated the view of her breasts rising and falling. Fact was, he appreciated most everything about Linette Clayton.

"I started asking questions around town. There is no labor problem. The miners work for slave's wages and don't care. Many of them steal from the mines, smuggling gold nuggets out to make ends meet."

"We knew that," Slocum said.

"What I found out was most interesting. Henry Hackett is having financial problems with the Iron-Silver Mining Company, and the Colorado Prince Mine isn't as profitable as it once was—so Carter Stevenson *does* run the best mine in Leadville."

"Hackett wants him dead so he can take it over?" Slocum shook his head. "Claim jumping on that big a scale isn't done. We're talking about big companies with offices in Denver, not half-crazy, starving prospectors who've been out in the hills too long. No one would ever honor Hackett's claim to any of the Little Pittsburgh Mining Company property."

"They would if he already owned a part of the mine—and was on the board of directors."

"Does Stevenson know this?" Slocum frowned. The man wasn't exactly a genius, but he had a certain cunning about him that hinted how he had become owner of the Little Pittsburgh Mine.

"He might not. It seems Hackett used an alias to buy a few shares of the Little Pittsburgh Mine. Not many, but enough. And he and Stevenson are on each other's boards of directors."

"That's not unusual," Slocum said. "There are only so many men out here with any knowledge of running a large mining operation."

"That may be," Linette admitted, "but Henry Hackett is in the position to take over the Little Pittsburgh Mining Company if anything happened to Carter Stevenson. And there have been other deaths of mine owners."

"Did Hackett buy into them after their owners were murdered?"

"Nobody thinks the three owners were murdered," Linette said. "They died under mysterious circumstances but . . ."

"Mining is dangerous," Slocum finished. "So three others are dead and Hackett had moved in on their claims?"

"Yes!"

"And you think he's moving in on Stevenson, too? How does this tie in with killing your sister and the officers of his own company?"

"My sister was an innocent bystander," Linette said, a tear welling at the corner of her bright blue eyes. "Hackett wanted Rupert Norton and the others dead. She just got in the way."

"Hackett wanted total control of the Iron-Silver Mining Company, but that's not enough for him," said Slocum. "He wants more, lots more."

"He wants it all, the greedy pig!"

He looked up into her eyes and saw the passion there. It wasn't the right time to tell her to just let it be and move on. Truth to tell, Slocum wasn't inclined to leave Leadville now, either. He didn't owe Carter Stevenson anything. He had saved the man's life once when he thwarted the ambush Griff and Harrison had set up. But he did owe himself something.

If he just left Leadville, the knowledge of a murdering Griff—and Henry Hackett—would ride with him. Slocum knew he couldn't live with that. He had to finish the job he'd started. For himself.

And for Linette.

She bent over, her red lips brushing across his. Slocum started to roll onto his back, but the woman's surging desire wasn't to be denied by even this simple move. She pressed down on top of him, her lips hungrily seeking his. They kissed until both panted for air.

She pushed away just long enough to begin unfastening her dress. If she had looked like a Sunday school teacher before, she was the complete opposite now. Linette's eyes

sparkled with wanton lust. She licked her lips and made it
so sensual that Slocum felt himself hardening at the sight.

"Hurry," he said.

"Help me." She bent forward, her breasts pressing up
and out of her half-fastened blouse. His fingers worked along
the laces holding everything together. He lingered for a
moment as he felt the soft, warm flesh. Linette sighed and
closed her eyes.

Slocum's hands dipped farther down her neckline. She
gasped when his fingers caught the hard, penny-colored
nipple and squeezed down. He felt her heart beating through
the pebble of flesh. He started rolling the left nipple in tiny
circles. Linette moaned constantly, her body swaying in
tempo with his manhandling.

"More, John. I need more than this." Her own fingers
stroked over his belly, then dipped even lower. She stroked
the hardness between his legs. The thick denim trousers got
in the way. Slocum felt trapped as the woman's eager hand
worked on him.

He got her blouse open and exposed the twin, melon-
sized mounds of whiteness. He strained his neck getting his
lips to the left nipple. His tongue worked on the hard button,
then moved to the other one. He tried to push the nipple
all the way into the soft flesh behind it. Every attempt
failed—and every attempt made Linette even hotter.

She fumbled at his belt and almost ripped his pants off
when she got his fly unbuttoned. The long, hard shaft of
manhood poking up made her shiver in anticipation.

"I want it," she said softly, her eyes fixed on the turgid
tip. Then she did to him what he had been doing to her
nipples.

Slocum lay back on the bed and let the soft, wet sensations
wash over him. He drifted, then floated. He became a cloud
high in the blue sky, but no cloud had ever been so stim-
ulated. He soared.

"Not yet," he muttered. "I want more," he said to her. He was fighting back the hot tide of his rising passion. Linette's clever mouth touched all the spots that roused him the most.

"More? What more could you possibly want?" she teased. She eluded his grasping hands and danced back, spinning around. As the dark-haired woman moved, the blouse came free. She stood naked to the waist. The light from the coal-oil lamp lit her body, hiding delectable portions and highlighting others.

"I want you," he said. "Now."

She laughed joyously. Linette tugged at her skirt and gave a wiggle that made Slocum even harder as he watched. She stepped out of her skirt and petticoats. In another second she was totally naked. Her body gleamed in the flickering yellow light and turned her into a wild and carefree spirit.

Slocum jumped off the bed and caught her up in his arms. A quick sweep took the woman off her feet. She threw her arms around his neck and let him turn and put her gently onto the bed. He slipped onto the bed beside her, bonfire-hot for what she had to offer.

"This is so natural, John. Promise me you'll never leave me."

"Let's finish, then we can talk. I've got better uses for my mouth. And so do you." His lips crushed hers. Linette threw her arms around his neck and kept him close. He felt her fingernails beginning to rake his back. He hardly noticed as his own appetites mounted. Slocum needed the release Linette gave him. He needed her.

He might even need her love.

Her fingers stroked over his chest, tangled in the mat of hair she found there, then moved lower. It was his turn to gasp when her fingers tightened around him. She started stroking. Again he felt as if she played with fire near a stick of dynamite.

"No more. Not like this," he said. His hands stroked over her belly, then went lower. He parted her alabaster thighs, revealing the moist, dark, furry triangle between them. She guided him directly to the spot they both desired to be filled with his throbbing shaft.

Slocum paused for a moment as the tip of his prong touched the woman's soft nether lips. He looked down into her eyes, then bent forward a bit and kissed her. At the same time his hips swung forward.

Linette tensed beneath him as he invaded her inner fastness. Then he pulled back and she went berserk. Her body thrashed around in desire for him. He held on and kept stroking, slowly at first, then with increasing need. Holding back became impossible.

His hips exploded in a wild, frenzied motion that burned both of them and set fire to their innards. Slocum didn't even try to slow the outward rush of his hot seed. Linette groaned and gasped and arched her back as he pumped harder and harder.

"Oh, yes, John, yes, yes!" She clutched at him again. He felt the sting of her nails this time. In a few seconds she shuddered like a leaf in a high wind, then settled down, sweaty and satisfied.

He looked down into her eyes again and saw the utter contentment there. She felt the same about him as he did her. He read it in her expression.

"Linette," he started. Slocum stopped talking and pushed himself back from her.

"What's wrong, John?"

"I don't know. I thought I heard something."

"It's just the wind. There might be a storm brewing over the mountains."

He was about to agree when he saw movement at the window. Slocum pushed himself away from Linette as hard as he could. He crashed to the floor just as the window exploded in a shower of glass shards. Slocum grabbed for his holstered six-shooter when the second blast from the shotgun came through the window.

"Linette!" he cried.

Sightless blue eyes stared at him. The buckshot had caught her square in the chest.

14

Slocum was stunned at the sight of Linette Clayton lying on the bed where they had just made love. He reached over and touched her cheek, thinking this would revive her. She didn't stir. He pressed his fingers into the side of her throat, vainly searching for a pulse.

She had been foully murdered.

Rage seized Slocum. He gave forth a maddened roar, then exploded into action. His ebony-handled Colt would avenge his lover's death. He swung across the small hotel room, oblivious to the glass on the floor cutting his bare feet. The muzzle of his six-shooter preceded him as he went out the window.

Slocum almost died as he burst out onto the balcony. His anger had boiled over and erased his usual good sense. Griff stood at the corner of the balcony, shotgun resting against the side of the battered building. When Slocum showed himself, the mine foreman squeezed off another shot. Double-ought buck ripped along the wood wall, sending splinters and death flying everywhere.

Slocum started firing even as he threw himself flat. The

flight of lead shot missed him—and he missed Griff. A second barrel from the sawed-off shotgun came closer to ending Slocum's life. He winced as white-hot lead seared his left arm.

He kept firing until the hammer fell on an empty cylinder.

By then his blood rage had eased, and Griff was long gone. He stood and stared at the end of the balcony—and past. Lights in Leadville danced just beyond. Stars twinkled merrily in the cold, crisp Rocky Mountain night air. It didn't seem like the proper setting for such bloody death.

Slocum looked over the railing when he heard people in the street below. Only when several of the men guffawed did he realize that he had dived through the window without a stitch of clothing on. He didn't have any false modesty, but being without pants made him feel vulnerable. Slocum ducked back into the hotel room.

Almost against hope, he checked for a beating in Linette's heart. Her breasts were beginning to turn cold. Nothing he could do would bring her back. The blast had caught her dead in the chest, snuffing her life out instantly.

Griff—and Henry Hackett—had robbed him of something more important than his own life. Even if they didn't have other crimes to be called on, this one demanded their deaths. Slowly. Painfully. Slocum wouldn't rest until Linette was avenged.

He pulled on his clothes, knowing he could never return to this room. He settled the cross-draw holster until it rode just right. He wasn't going to meet Griff again and not be armed and ready. Then he sat on the edge of the bed and reloaded his pistol.

Every round that went into every cylinder caused a new icicle to form in his gut. Any of the bullets might be the one that ended Griff's foul, back-shooting life.

Or all of them. He might just empty the six-shooter into the mine foreman's gut.

"Open up. What's going on it there?" came an aggrieved cry from the hall. The night clerk banged on the door again. Slocum ignored him. He gathered his belongings, packed them into his saddlebags, then paused to stare down at Linette's still form.

He bent and gently kissed her one last time. Then he spun and stalked to the door, his duty clear.

"What's been going on?" the clerk said. He peered past Slocum and went pale.

"She was shot through the window by a shotgun," Slocum said by way of explanation.

"There's no sheriff," the clerk muttered.

"It doesn't matter. I'll take care of it myself." Slocum shoved past the clerk and went to the street. One man recognized Slocum as the man who had been naked on the balcony. He pointed him out to his friends. They all began laughing.

The laughter died when they saw the bleakness and sheer meanness in Slocum's eyes.

He climbed onto the porch and addressed the small crowd. "Griff just killed a woman. I want him." A murmur passed through the crowd. A few at the edges drifted away, not wanting any part of this crazy man's vengeance. Others, more sheeplike, crowded together for comfort and protection from this elemental force.

"Where do I find him?" Slocum's green eyes shone like polar ice as they worked across the crowd. No one moved. They were all frozen by his stare.

From the rear of the rabble came a small voice. "I saw him an hour ago at the Big Colorado Saloon."

Slocum didn't bother to thank the man for this tidbit of information. It was where he would have looked first. He walked down the steps from the porch. The crowd parted in front of him and re-formed behind. Slocum might have

been a winter storm blowing through Leadville. Men
stepped back in fear when he passed.

He didn't even break stride as he walked into the Big
Colorado Saloon. The doors slammed hard against the walls
and caused a silence to fall on the miners in the saloon. The
whore who had tried to give him the knockout drops earlier
bolted and ran when she saw him. Slocum's hand whipped
to his pistol. He drew and cocked it in a smooth movement.
The muzzle pointed straight at the barkeep, who was reaching for a weapon under the bar.

"Griff. I want him. Where is he?"

"I don't know, mister. Honest!"

Slocum let the hammer down, started to replace his six-
shooter, then swung the pistol back hard. He caught the
barkeep on the side of the head, sending the man to the
floor. An ax handle dropped from the man's numbed fingers.

The low murmur in the room died entirely as Slocum
made his way through. Men who would have tried to pick
a fight before left him alone now. Only death met anyone
crossing Slocum this night, and the miners sensed it.

Slocum went to the door leading to the back room. He
had seen the whore enter there. She must know where Griff
was or she wouldn't have fled. Slocum kicked in the door
and followed his drawn pistol into the room.

The darkness wrapped him like a shroud. He edged into
the room, wary of an ambush. Slocum found the rear door.
It had been barred on the inside, and the heavy iron rod
still locked it into place. No one had left this room. The
whore was still around somewhere.

Slocum found an oil lamp. Six-shooter ready in his right
hand, he fumbled in his shirt pocket for a lucifer. He struck
it and the phosphorus flared whitely. Slocum knocked the
mantle off the lamp. It shattered with a tinkling sound. The
wick needed trimming, but Slocum wasn't after good-qual-
ity light.

The guttering flame cast shadows around the room. He held the lamp high and turned slowly. He stopped when he saw a human silhouette cast on the far wall of the storeroom.

"Where is Griff?" Slocum said.

"Don't kill me, mister. I don't know nothing. It's all Griff's doing, whatever it is that's got you so riled."

She was lying and Slocum knew it. He went to her and towered above her. She was a pathetic figure, but he had no mercy or sympathy left. It had all died with Linette Clayton.

Slocum sloshed some of the coal oil from the lamp onto the woman's hair. She flinched back.

"Where is Griff?" he repeated. She began to cry. He lowered the lamp until the flickering light threatened to spit sparks and ignite her oil-soaked hair.

"I don't know!" she shrieked, cowering. Slocum pushed the lamp closer. This time he didn't threaten. She knew what the penalty would be for lying.

"Honest! He was here earlier. He said he had business. He'd just been paid to do it. He don't tell me nothing! He left and I ain't seen him since. Please, mister. The fire's gonna—"

Slocum threw the oil lamp against the wall with all his might. Oil spattered everything in the room. He spun on his heel and went back to the saloon's main room. He said nothing as he passed back through. By the time he reached the front door, the whore's shrieks echoed from the back room.

No one moved to help her. When the thick black smoke began billowing into the saloon, a stampede started. Slocum paused halfway down the street and saw the Big Colorado in flames. He didn't know if the whore had escaped. It didn't matter much to him. The emptiness inside would never go away.

Where would he find Griff? The fire would drive him

away like the rat he was. Slocum knew he might have wasted an opportunity to find the bloodthirsty killer. Now Griff would be on his guard—and probably taken to ground once more to weather the storm.

Slocum vowed that this was one storm Griff wouldn't survive. But how was he to find him, especially if Griff was able to hide behind Henry Hackett's expensive coat-tails?

Only one possible ally suggested himself to Slocum. He started down the street, his steps moving inexorably toward the Leadville Trotting and Racing Club. Carter Stevenson was involved in this fiasco up to his ears, too. It was time he did something more than get drunk and put bets on the horses.

The bouncers at the door hesitated when he came up. One had been on duty when he had entered with Stevenson after the abortive attempt on the mine owner's life. Doubt crossed the man's face; he wasn't sure of Slocum's station. He was even less sure he ought to let anyone into the ex-clusive club who had blood in his eye.

"Can we help you, sir?" the bouncer asked.

"I want to talk to Mr. Stevenson. Is he in the club?" Slocum looked up the side of the brick building at the top floor. He remembered eating there. He remembered finding Linette there with Henry Hackett. If possible, he went even colder inside at the memory.

"I believe he is. Locke, go ask."

The other bouncer nodded once, then vanished inside. Slocum stood on the front steps, seething at the wait. He wanted everything done—and done *now*. Every second he wasted gave Griff an extra mile or two head start. But he needed Stevenson's help. Without it, Griff could hide behind Hackett's money forever.

"You been back in town?" asked the bouncer.

"Came from that direction," Slocum said.

"What's the big fire? Looks as if half of Leadville is on fire."

"Might be," Slocum said, not wanting to say anything more. He had started the fire. Let Hackett put it out.

"These towns are all made of clapboard and prayer. I was over in Cripple Creek a year or so back. Fire damn near burned the place to the ground. Hell of a blaze."

"This one will be, too," Slocum said. He was more interested in Locke returning. The man's smile reassured Slocum that everything was all right. Locke had found Stevenson and gotten permission to let the murderous-looking man into the Leadville Trotting and Racing Club.

"Go on in," said Locke. "Mr. Stevenson is on the third floor, in the salon."

"I'll find it." Slocum pushed into the posh club and went up the stairs, taking them two at a time. To his right he saw a dimly lit room with waiters hovering near the few men seated in overstuffed chairs. Near a fireplace sat Carter Stevenson, drinking a snifter of brandy and smoking a huge cigar.

Slocum went over to him. Stevenson looked up, his eyes clear and sharp. His voice came out slightly muzzy, as if he had been drinking heavily all day.

"Wha' kin I do for you, Mr. Slocum?" Stevenson belched and put his hand to his mouth. He pushed himself up in the chair and took a tighter rein on himself. "Sit down. Sorry to be so—"

Slocum didn't let him find the proper words. He planted himself squarely in the chair next to Stevenson's and leaned forward, hands on his knees.

"She's dead, Stevenson. Linette Clayton is dead."

"Who? Oh, the woman with Hackett. That's a pity. She was a lovely girl." Stevenson's clear eyes sharpened even more and pierced Slocum's soul. "She meant more to you than that, didn't she?"

"Her sister, Angelica, was the one killed at the wedding massacre in Denver."

"The pieces begin fitting together," Stevenson said. He sipped at his brandy, puffed a bit more on his cigar, sending huge blue clouds of smoke into the room, then leaned back. "You know how she died?"

"She was murdered. Hackett's foreman, Griff, pulled the trigger. He shotgunned her just as he did her sister."

"Hackett will have to answer for this, of course." Stevenson puffed once more on the cigar, then stubbed it out in a brass pot of sand next to his chair. "There's no marshal in these parts, though. Getting the law in from Denver isn't going to be easy. They don't rightly care what happens in Leadville. Can't say I blame them much, either. This is a wild and lawless place, and Denver has its own problems."

"Griff did it. Hackett ordered the killing, just as he ordered Griff and Harrison to bushwhack you."

"Harrison?"

"One of the hombres who rode with Griff."

"Your words suggest he has taken off for parts unknown."

"He's dead," Slocum said brutally. The sharp words didn't ruffle Stevenson any. He nodded and sipped at his brandy, looking at Slocum over the snifter's crystal rim.

"You killed him?"

"No, someone else did. He saved my life doing it. But I lost track of Griff and he got away from me." Slocum's expression turned even more dour. If he had gunned down Griff before the foreman had escaped into the mine shaft, Linette might still be alive.

"Who aided you by removing this, uh, scum?"

"I don't know."

"Pity. We might need all the help we can get."

Slocum was glad to hear Stevenson's words. The mine

owner was beginning to think about helping bring Hackett to justice.

"You know Hackett was the one behind the attempt on your life?" asked Slocum.

"Of course I do. No one shoots at me without arousing some speck of curiosity. If nothing else, I don't want them doing it again—when you're not around. No, Mr. Slocum, I know who has been killing off the other mine owners."

"Linette figured it out, too."

"She did? How?"

"It's not hard. All the bloody trails stop at Hackett's feet. His mine isn't producing as much silver as it once did. Debts pile up. Greed expands faster than any mine can deliver ingots."

"Yes, there is that," Stevenson said, a faraway look in his eye. "There is always greed." He finished the brandy in a gulp and signaled the waiter for more. Slocum shook his head when Stevenson silently invited him to join in another snifter.

"I want Griff and I want Hackett. As far as I'm concerned, they're both equally guilty."

"The blood is on both sets of hands," agreed Stevenson. "A pity about your Linette. Such a fine-looking girl, so pretty and bright and alive."

The words worked like a nettle under his saddle blanket. Slocum shifted uneasily in the chair. The need for action called even louder to him now than it had before.

"I need your help. Hackett's too rich and powerful for me to go up against alone. He tried to kill you. And you said you knew he'd murdered three other mine owners."

"Three? I never said three," Stevenson contended. "I know of at least four and suspect one or two more. All appeared to be accidents. Mine-shaft collapses, accidents with dynamite, one was run over by a loaded ore cart—

those kind of unprovable accidents. Hackett is a dangerous fellow."

"Linette said the board of directors for Iron-Silver and the Little Pittsburgh Mining Companies interlock. And she also said Hackett had bought stock in your company under an alias, trying to work his way in and take control anonymously."

For the first time Slocum got a rise out of Carter Stevenson. The man's eyebrows shot up. He drained his brandy in a long gulp and put it down firmly. Whatever trace of drunkenness that Slocum had seen when he approached Stevenson was long gone now.

"The son of a bitch. I didn't know that." Stevenson's lips thinned to a grim line.

"He wants you dead so he can take over."

"Greed. He wants more than the best mines in Leadville. That son of a bitch wants them all!"

Slocum saw that he had a firm ally in Carter Stevenson. All he had to do now was make the alliance work.

15

"We have come to a crossroads," Carter Stevenson said pompously. "The time has come for action, not words." He reached into his jacket pocket and pulled out a wallet thick with greenbacks. Riffling through them, he handed a stack to Slocum.

"What's this for?" Slocum asked. Stevenson had given him more than five hundred dollars. This was a princely sum, even if it was paper money.

"A retainer. You now work for me."

"I don't need this."

"Keep it, keep it," Stevenson said, waving his hand as if he were swatting at an annoying fly. "You'll earn it and more if you catch Griff."

"What about Henry Hackett?"

"I'll take care of my good friend, Mr. Hackett," Stevenson said. "He travels in circles beyond your reach, I fear. Even with that much in your pocket, Hackett commands vast hordes of minions. Harrison died. Griff can find a hundred more like him with Henry's money to back him up in the recruiting."

"The third one who shot up the wedding is dead, too," Slocum said. "I killed him in Denver."

Again Stevenson showed his surprise. He covered it well. "You are an ambitious man, Mr. Slocum. I appreciate that. We will work through this knotty problem together and come out on the other side. Mark my words, Henry Hackett will positively rue the day he thought to take over *my* mine!"

Slocum said nothing. Money—greed—wasn't what kept him moving toward the deaths of Griff and the murderous fat man, Henry Hackett. It was simply vengeance for robbing him of the only thing that had mattered to him in years.

Even those men's deaths wouldn't bring back Linette. It might not even make Slocum feel any better, but it would go a long way toward settling the score. They wouldn't inflict their brand of treachery and deceit on anyone else.

"Where is Hackett likely to be?"

"Leave him to me." Stevenson pointed to the greenbacks still clutched in Slocum's hand. "Use those wisely."

"What about Griff?"

"Ah, Hackett's foreman is another matter. He often spends considerable time in the Big Colorado Saloon. Do you know where this establishment is?"

"He's not there," Slocum said. "I just burned it to the ground to be sure."

"Indeed, Mr. Slocum. I have underestimated you. I'll try not to do it again. The only other locale where Griff would feel safe is in the mine where he and Harrison tried to waylay you."

"I'll need someone who knows the area. Who do I see?"

"Alas, that poses something of a problem. No one knows the area as well as Griff. He is a competent miner and his father was an even better one. The man grew up in the mines."

Slocum frowned. He didn't cotton to the notion of following Griff underground. "He's safer in a mine shaft," he admitted. "He only has to watch in two directions."

"Don't be gulled into thinking he is an unimaginative man, either. Be wary of traps, Mr. Slocum."

Slocum heaved himself to his feet. He had a vicious sidewinder to track down. He found himself wanting to be as far away from Leadville as possible. The sooner he started after Griff, the sooner it would be over.

Slocum slipped his foot out of the stirrup and curled his leg around the pommel. He leaned forward. He had ridden slowly through the night, biding his time, waiting for dawn. He wasn't even sure Griff had come this way, but something in his gut told him Stevenson had been right. This was where the foreman would run.

The mouth of the mine shaft gaped open not a quarter mile from where he sat on his gelding. The tailings looked like vomit spewing forth—and Slocum had to go inside if he wanted Griff.

"Might just blow the tunnel," he said, thinking aloud. He knew this wouldn't work. He had to be sure Griff was inside before he did that. Even a good-sized explosion might not be adequate to the task. These mines ran for miles underground. There might be a dozen other exits Griff could use to escape.

Slocum had to be sure the man was dead, dead, dead.

He hiked his leg over the top and slid to the ground. The horse nickered softly. He patted the animal on the neck, then led the horse toward the mine. He found a stand of scrub oak with a patch of grass large enough to keep the horse happy for a few hours.

Tethering the gelding, Slocum unfastened the thong on the hammer of his pistol. He was ready to see if Griff had returned there.

The path to the mine opening was littered with small

stones and debris from the mining operation. Dark ore showed where silver telluride had been in the earth. His sharp eyes looked for any sign that someone had preceded him.

Slocum found no hint that Griff was inside. Even so, the hair on the back of his neck rose when he moved to the mine opening. Dawn was breaking and outlined him, making him a sitting duck for a man with a shotgun.

Slocum let out a low sigh of relief when no fiery tongues of flame licked forth, signaling the onslaught of deadly buckshot. Just inside the opening, he paused and studied the timbers. They were rickety and hadn't been replaced in years. He had come this way before and decided against pursuing Griff.

He had no choice now. Slocum entered the mine, the mouth getting smaller behind him as he advanced. The shaft floor still carried twin iron rails, long since rusted away. He had to step carefully to keep from stumbling over them in the dark.

As he went, he looked for the small ledges along the walls where long-gone miners would have stored candles. Just before the light from the dawn-lit opening vanished, he found a small cache of candles. Even better, a carbide lantern lay on its side on the floor. Slocum shook it hard and was pleased to hear water sloshing inside.

Pumping hard at the piston, he got the lantern lit. The carbide needed replacing, but it was better than trying to carry a candle. The lantern wasn't as likely to go out on him should shooting start. Just to be sure, though, Slocum put several candle stubs into his pocket against possible lantern failure.

The carbide lantern hissed and made Slocum strain to hear any movement from deeper in the mine. He walked for several minutes before coming to a drift running at right angles to the main shaft. He cursed. Which way would Griff have gone?

Slocum knelt and studied the shaft's filthy floor. The loose stones and debris made it impossible to guess if anyone had passed through in the past two years, much less the last few hours. Slocum held the carbide lantern up and checked over the jagged rock walls. A slow smile crossed his face. At just about belt level he saw a metallic scratch better than six inches long.

Closer examination showed it to be from a rifle—or shotgun—barrel.

"Got you, you stinking bastard," Slocum muttered.

He tread more cautiously now, careful not to make any loud noises that might echo along the tunnel and warn Griff he had company. There wasn't much he could do about the lantern; Slocum needed the light it cast. Without it he might fall into a stope.

Even as the thought crossed his mind he stopped at the edge of a deep pit. Miners had worked a silver vein straight down for almost a hundred feet. Slocum corrected himself. Miners had worked up from a lower level. It was easier to let the drilled rock fall past than it was to dig it and have to heave it up out of an excavation.

Easing around the stope, he continued along the drift. Slocum stopped after a few more minutes and looked behind. He had a vague sense that something wasn't quite right. The rocky tunnel wasn't cut straight. It curved slightly, blocking off a view of the stope.

Slocum put down the lantern, drew his pistol, and backtracked cautiously. Over the years he had developed an acute sixth sense about danger. It well nigh screamed now—and he wasn't going to ignore it. The niggling, scratchy sensation at the back of his brain had kept him alive too many times.

It worked for him again.

Rocks tumbled from the stope going up into the hillside. Someone was working his way down to the shaft where Slocum waited.

Slocum didn't have to look to know who was coming down. It had to be Griff.

Slocum wedged himself into a small niche, designed for miners to avoid the ore cart as it passed by on the tracks. He wasn't in any hurry, and neither was Griff. The mine foreman swore a blue streak as he bumped and bounced off the rugged walls of the vertical shaft. Showers of dirt and dust came down, obscuring everything in the mine.

Slocum's nose twitched. He forced back the sneeze that might have betrayed his position. Griff acted as if he were alone. Slocum wanted to keep the advantage of surprise as long as he could.

Until he squeezed off the round that ended the ugly bushwhacker's life.

Griff landed heavily in the tunnel, grunted, and swung a burlap bag over his shoulder. He came through the dust looking like the boogey man in a child's nightmare. Slocum shifted slightly and poked out of the niche.

He might have disturbed a stone and Griff heard it. Or he might have seen the lantern down the tunnel. Or the man might have a sixth sense about danger, like Slocum. Whatever the reason, he bent forward and dropped his sack in front of him.

Slocum saw Griff going for his pistol. Slocum didn't have time to sight properly. He loosed a round in the foreman's direction, hoping to hit something important. He heard his slug whistle off metal in the pack.

"Who is it?" shouted Griff. "Who's there?"

"Your executioner," Slocum said coldly. He shifted to the far side of the tunnel for a better shot. Griff backed away, putting the slight curve in the shaft between him and Slocum.

Slocum knew better than to shoot blindly. His vision was obscured by the cloaking dust Griff had kicked up, and the bend in the tunnel. Even worse, too many loud reports might bring the tunnel collapsing all around him. The timbers hadn't been repaired in years. Termites had found more than one good meal in the roof supports, and just banging into one wall support convinced Slocum he was in a death trap.

He wanted it to be a death trap—but only for Griff.

"Who is it? Why are you after me?" the foreman screeched. Slocum knew he had him spooked. That was good. If Griff panicked, he'd get careless.

Slocum dropped to his belly and crawled forward through the choking dust. He had a rusty spike poking him in the tender side by the time he scooted around the bend in the tunnel. He saw a faint outline. He fired. The silhouette moved rapidly, and Slocum knew he had missed.

More dust and rock fell in a cloud over him. Slocum realized the gunfight couldn't last too long or they'd both be entombed for eternity. This mine was slowly caving in all around him.

"Go away. I don't want anything to do with you. I was only doing what Mr. Hackett told me to do."

Slocum retreated and got his carbide lantern. He turned down the illumination until it was only a ghostly glow. Holding it far to one side with his left hand, he returned to the stope from which Griff had descended from above. Slocum checked out the rocky ledges and saw that the foreman had a small living space in a recess fifteen feet above the tunnel floor. The bushwhacker wasn't likely to return to it, Slocum knew.

He stumbled over the sack Griff had dropped. Putting the lantern on the floor, Slocum checked the sack. He found a dozen sticks of dynamite, fuses, and blasting caps. The dynamite was safe; the fulminate of mercury blasting caps might detonate if he looked cross-eyed at them. Still, this was a treasure trove. Griff would *never* leave the mine alive now, not with such explosive power in Slocum's control.

Slocum took part of the string used to fasten shut the sack and looped it through his belt so he could drag the sack. He held the lantern to his side and clutched the Colt Navy in the other. He went hunting for Griff again.

The dust cleared, and he found a new stretch of tunnel. He stopped for a moment to get his bearings. He was getting turned around. He should have found the mouth of the mine leading back outside. Instead he saw a half dozen stopes plunging far into the ground. They had been drilled from any of five lower levels. Several were equipped with iron bars welded into crude ladders to allow the miners to enter and leave the different layers in the mine. Nowhere did Slocum see good, untapped veins of ore. The mine had petered out a long time ago.

He edged around the stopes and found himself in a dead end. He cursed his bad luck. Griff had descended to a lower level. Which stope had he taken? Where was the man?

Slocum studied the makeshift iron ladders and found one with scratches on it. Since the bright marks hadn't rusted over like others on the same ladder, he decided these were fresh. But he had no way of knowing how far down Griff had gone.

Going after the man didn't appeal to Slocum one iota, but he saw no way of flushing his quarry.

Unless . . .

Slocum rummaged in the sack until he came out with a stick of dynamite, a fuse, and a blasting cap. He squatted on the edge of the pit and prepared the explosive. He made sure his hands were visible in the light from the lantern, but his body was away from the lip. He wanted Griff to know what he planned—and to panic.

He crimped down the blasting cap using his teeth, forced

the cap and black fuse into the top of the stick, and then yelled, "It's got a thirty-second fuse on it, Griff."

Slocum stuck the fuse into the carbide flame and set it to sputtering. He paused for a moment, hoping the man was nearby. If he had hit the lower levels and run into this rabbit warren, there might be no finding him. Even worse, he might know other ways out of the mine. Slocum could be risking his own life for nothing.

"Don't!" Griff shouted. "You'll kill both of us."

"After what you did to Linette Clayton that might not be such a bad idea. I'd die happy knowing you were going to burn in hell, too!"

"Who? The woman in the hotel room? I didn't mean to shoot her. I was after you."

"That makes me feel real kindly toward you," Slocum said. He hadn't figured out where Griff was below him. He judged about fifteen seconds remained on the fuse. He dropped the stick.

The sputtering black fuse looked like a Catherine wheel in the darkness as it fell. It crashed into a floor thirty feet below. Slocum edged around to the side of the stope, away from the lantern so he wouldn't afford Griff a good target. Then he waited.

The fuse burned down to less than five seconds. This was when Griff rushed out and made a wild grab for the deadly red stick of dynamite.

Slocum bided his time and took careful aim. Firing downhill was always tricky, and the light wasn't too good in the mine. But he had determination on his side. He squeezed the Colt's trigger and the six-shooter bucked in his hand.

Griff let out an agonized cry. Slocum peered down the stope and saw the wounded foreman fall flat on his face next to the dynamite. He managed to grab the stick and pluck the fuse free before it set off the blasting cap.

"You murderin' bastard!" shouted Griff. "You busted

my leg with your shot, and you damn near killed me with the dynamite!''

"I never liked doing things half measure," Slocum said. He stood and looked down at Griff. The man struggled to get to his own pistol. Slocum fired three times, each bullet lodging in the foreman. Two broke his right arm. The third thudded into his damaged leg. He wasn't going anywhere— and he wasn't going to do much fighting back.

"I'm hurting. You got me fair and square. You can't leave me like this to die in the dark!''

"I'm not going to leave you like this," Slocum said. He went to the sack and made a bundle of the remaining five sticks of dynamite. He fixed another blasting cap and put a ten-foot fuse on it. He made certain Griff saw the bundle being placed at one side of the pit. Slocum strung the fuse across to the other side.

"What'n hell are you doing? Get me out of here. I'm bleedin' to death!''

"You won't bleed to death," Slocum assured him. He finished his preparation. The fuse dangled across the pit so Griff could see it.

He stuck the end of the black fuse into the carbide flame. The fuse sizzled and popped, then began to burn at its measured rate of one foot per minute.

"I figure you've got about ten minutes," Slocum said. "The fuse will fall down into the stope. You might try climbing up the ladder to put it out.''

"I can't. You busted my goddamn leg and my arm's all shot up.''

"Then you can watch the fuse burning toward the five sticks of dynamite.''

"You can't leave me like this!''

"Start climbing," Slocum said. He stared at the wounded man. Griff tried to pull himself up but failed. He slid back down to the floor of the mine's lower level. He looked up, wild-eyed and pleading.

Slocum turned and left. There was still nine feet of fuse left. Griff might be able to get up the ladder and pluck it out, but Slocum doubted it.

Using the lantern, he found where he had taken the wrong turn. He retraced his steps to the mouth of the mine. He turned off the carbide lantern and tossed the candle stubs in his pocket onto the mine floor. Checking his watch, he saw he had taken almost five minutes to get out of the shaft.

Slocum moved downslope, found a rock, and pulled out his fixings. He licked along one side of the rolling paper, then tapped out enough tobacco for a good smoke. He'd just lit it and taken a deep puff when a huge gout of rock and dust and noise belched from the mouth of the mine.

Slocum finished his smoke, then tossed the butt toward the closed mine. Griff wasn't going to use his sawed-off shotgun on any more innocent women.

16

Slocum rode slowly back toward Leadville, considering his future. There wasn't anything in the silver mining town to keep him there, even through the night. He had done what he could to avenge Angelica Clayton's death—and Linette's.

It didn't seem to be enough.

"Hackett," he muttered, unfulfilled in his revenge. "He's the mastermind. He's the one who deserved to be buried at the bottom of a deserted mine shaft." Slocum didn't even consider Griff's last few minutes of life, the terror that must have caused his heart to race until it almost burst, the sight of the fuse burning toward the dynamite, the last split second when realization of his own death came. Whatever he had done to Griff had been deserved. The man had been a cold-blooded murderer.

Henry Hackett wasn't any better. He paid Griff and Harrison and the other man to shoot up the wedding. All he wanted was to eliminate some of the competition for control of the Iron-Silver Mining Company. The more officers who died, the more of the company he controlled personally. He might as well have pulled the triggers that killed so many.

Hackett had to pay too. Slocum knew that even then revenge would taste like ash on his tongue. Nothing could bring back those so foully murdered. The best he could do was make the guilty pay.

Carter Stevenson was the tool he would use to make Hackett and any others who had helped him pay—with their lives.

Determined, Slocum put his heels to the gelding's flanks. The animal snorted and tossed its head, eager to be free of its anxious rider. Slocum rode quickly down the main street in Leadville, cold eyes never straying from the four-story brick building at the far end of town. The luxurious Leadville Trotting and Racing Club was Stevenson's unofficial headquarters. Slocum would find him there and learn what had happened with Hackett.

He never broke stride as he walked into the club. The two guards at the door eyed each other. The one named Locke shook his head slightly, as if saying, "I'm not messing with him."

Slocum climbed the broad, polished wood staircase and went directly to the sitting room on the third floor, where he had last seen Carter Stevenson. The man still sat in the overstuffed chair. A cloud of blue smoke hung around his head as he puffed gently. And the snifter of brandy still sat on the side table. It was as if the mining magnate hadn't stirred as much as his little finger.

"He's dead," Slocum said. "I buried the son of a bitch alive in the mine."

"Indeed, Mr. Slocum. It seems I have misjudged you once more. You are not only an ambitious man with imagination but you are also one vindictive . . . gentleman." Stevenson smiled broadly. "I like that very much. I do."

"Can the chatter. What about Hackett?"

"Patience, Mr. Slocum, patience."

"Patience is for vultures. I want his ass."

"And you shall get it. *We* shall get it. I have made inquiries. Henry had taken to the hills, and he has done it in a big way. It is his usual method—running away from his problems."

"What's that mean?" Slocum was tired of the verbal jousting. He wanted Hackett's scalp. If he had to take Stevenson's along the way to get it, he would. He couldn't abide by a fat-assed mine owner who thought he could do everything from an easy chair.

"Henry has a small army with him and has holed up in an old mine near the Iron-Silver Mining Company claims."

"How many men does he have? A hundred? More?"

"Probably fewer than ten."

"Then it's no big problem."

Stevenson laughed and sipped at his brandy. "There's no hurry, Mr. Slocum. Henry's not going anywhere. A drink? Brandy? Whiskey?" Stevenson motioned and one of the ever-attentive waiters came over with a shot glass of whiskey.

Slocum knocked it back, not tasting it. The liquor was probably first rate. He was in no mood to appreciate it. The warmth it lent to his belly was nothing compared to the fire burning there. He wanted Henry Hackett. He *wanted* him.

"You'd take him on single-handed. That's foolhardy, Mr. Slocum." Stevenson seemed to be enjoying the banter. It was making Slocum increasing edgy. What game was Carter Stevenson playing?

"It was damn stupid for Hackett to order Linette and her sister and the others slaughtered like cattle, too."

"Ah, straight to the heart of the matter." Stevenson sobered and leaned forward. "If I offered you another five hundred dollars, would you forget this private vendetta of yours?"

"You want to pay me to stop?" Slocum's cold green eyes bored into Stevenson. He didn't understand the man's motives. "Hackett tried to have you gunned down. Are you letting up on him?"

"An answer, sir. Would five hundred dollars be enough to let your conscience rest easy?"

"I'll find him on my own." Slocum pushed to his feet and started to leave the posh club.

"Wait! I'm sorry, Mr. Slocum. I was testing you. I wanted to know that you were truly determined to carry through, no matter what happened. I am not offering you money for Hackett. I needed to know if your will could be bent."

Slocum glared at Stevenson. The mine owner seemed to wilt under the cold look.

"I know you much better now, sir. We will attack the problem together. In that way we can both come out triumphant. Please, Mr. Slocum, humor me."

"I want Hackett" was all Slocum said. Stevenson was playing some sort of game, thinking this was nothing more than a rich man's idle pursuit. He was wrong. Slocum wondered what good Stevenson would be when the bullets started flying. He hadn't seen the man's reaction after Harrison and Griff had shot up his carriage. He might have been pale and shaken.

Slocum hoped to hell that Stevenson didn't think they'd get out of this without pain and blood.

"I have a map prepared. We shall reconnoiter the area. You can give me the battle plans, and we can work from there."

"I'm not rushing into anything just because you've got a map," Slocum said. "Everything has to be right before we make our move."

"Exactly, my point, sir. Yes, well, let's look at the map. Where is it? Ah, yes, here." Stevenson motioned and the waiter brought a leather surveyor's map case and handed it over. Slocum waited impatiently for Stevenson to riffle through the sheaf of papers inside and find the proper plat.

"It won't be easy taking him," said Stevenson. His finger stabbed down on the map showing the highest elevation. "Here is his fortress. It is built from rock from a nearby mine. Ten men, perhaps one or two more. All the supplies they need to last through the winter. Yes, Hackett is ready for a siege."

Slocum studied the map. He couldn't tell much from the contour lines. He needed to see the lay of the land personally, but an idea slowly came to him. He didn't want Stevenson recruiting an army. One bunch of mercenaries fighting another was no good.

He wanted the pleasure of dealing with Henry Hackett himself.

"Who'd you get to help us? Some of your miners out at the Little Pittsburgh?"

"Who else? I pay them, and they are reasonably loyal. Not many of them cotton to Henry, either. I got some of my best men from him. He mistreats his workers horribly."

"They're not paid gunmen," Slocum said, more to himself than to Stevenson.

"I should say not."

"They won't be much good in a real fight. The first one that gets picked off will send the others scuttling back to their holes."

"They are brave men," said Stevenson. "They risk their lives to mine my ore!"

"I'm not saying they're not brave in that way. I've seen men face the damnedest things, then in battle freeze up. Those are the lucky ones. The others turn tail and run like scalded dogs."

"What do you suggest?"

"I'll need some explosives."

"That's no problem," Stevenson said, chuckling. "I've got storehouses filled with dynamite and caps. Do you want some fuse too?"

Slocum was in no mood to joke. He turned back to the map and got the canyons and rises firmly in his mind. Once he got out to Hackett's hideaway, he didn't intend having to waste time pulling out any damn surveyor's map.

Slocum peered through a small telescope Stevenson had given him. The field of vision wasn't enough to help him much. He wobbled a bit as he sighted through it, owing to the high wind whipping down off the Rockies. Slocum finally gave up and squinted toward the fortress, nestled in a rocky divide between two hills.

"Got a good place there. You have to approach from either this side or go all the way around and come at him along a mining road that runs down the valley. Might be more'n ten extra miles to go that way." Stevenson seemed inordinately proud of himself. He was decked out in British hunting gear, as if he were ready to ride to the hounds.

Slocum didn't want to tell him Henry Hackett was no fox—and there wasn't a pack of dogs on their side.

"I'm more interested in the tops of the hills," Slocum said.

"Can't get to them easily. There's no way of mounting an attack coming down those slopes. They are much too steep, Mr. Slocum. I had hoped you would have more military sense."

"This isn't going to be found in any book on maneuvers," Slocum said.

"Indeed. Enlighten me as to your course of action."

"Got the wagon loaded with the dynamite?"

"I have, sir. There's almost five hundred pounds. This is an extreme amount, even for that fortress."

Slocum had to agree. If he could just ride up to the front

and put the dynamite where it'd do the most good, he wouldn't need more than ten pounds to destroy Hackett's stronghold.

Hackett wouldn't take kindly to anyone doing that. By the time he'd reached the halfway point going up the road to the stone-walled fortress, he'd be sucking wind through a dozen new holes in his body.

"I'll need it. Why don't you go on back to town and let me handle this?" he said.

"We're in this together, sir. Really!"

"There's not a hell of a lot for you to do," Slocum said. He went to the wagon and heaved off three cases of dynamite. The rest he rearranged to ride more easily in the wagon bed. He had to circle the hills and come up the back way if he wanted to cut off Hackett's escape.

"What do you plan to do with the dynamite, Mr. Slocum? This is going to make a mighty big crater if it all goes off."

"I've handled dynamite before," Slocum said. He got into the wagon and put the reins to the team. The two horses shuddered and put their heads down and started pulling. It took almost a mile before Slocum got the rhythm of driving them and began the ten-mile drive around the hillside and up the back way.

As he rode, he went over his plan in his mind. It wasn't too complex but might be more difficult to carry out. He had to cut off Hackett's retreat. To do that he wanted one hellacious rock slide to seal the road and make climbing over it impossible. Damn near five hundred pounds of dynamite would open the side of a mountain like a hunting knife slicing through a fresh peach.

"Plant it right and Hackett's ass is mine," he said. Slocum pulled the team to a halt just after midday. The sun beat down fiercely. The higher altitudes made sunburn a serious problem. He pulled his hat lower and wiped some of the sweat off his face with a bandanna. Only then did he look up to see if he was close to the spot he had picked off the contour map.

A glint of sunlight off metal alerted Slocum to the sentry posted to watch the back way. He wondered if Hackett was spooked enough to go all out, or if he was sitting in his rock-walled fortress thinking he was safe and secure.

Losing Harrison and Griff might have decided him on a cautious approach to life.

Slocum dismounted and looked for the new rifle he had bought with some of Stevenson's money. He frowned as he checked it. The gun grease hadn't been completely cleaned from it. He worried that the bullet might not travel straight and true. He shrugged it off. He had been in a hurry to get out there and be done with Henry Hackett. This was the price he paid for such haste.

The wagon and its deadly load were just out of sight around a sharp curve in the road. Slocum tried to remember the exact spot where he wanted to place the dynamite. He couldn't bring the spot to mind; he'd have to take out the sentry and use the lofty perch to scout the spot where the explosive would do the most damage.

Moving steadily up the side of the hill proved easier than he had thought. The boulders littering the side of the knoll gave him more than enough cover. Slocum had just dropped to his knee and sighted up at the sentry when the man carelessly silhouetted himself against the sky.

The guard stretched and yawned widely, not paying any attention to what was going on less than twenty yards away. Slocum centered the front sight on the man's chest and started squeezing back on the trigger. He relaxed and ducked back when a voice was carried to him on the wind.

"Hey, Smoky, where the hell are you?"

The guard turned and waved. Slocum heaved a sigh for his good luck. Either two sentries were posted, or the relief had come to let Smoky go back to Hackett's fortress. If he had taken out the careless guard, the other would have been all over him like flies on shit.

"Over here. Can't see beans, but this is where Mr. Hackett told me to stay."

"Been in a game. Those poor fools don't know odds. I cleaned the lot of them out."

"Shoulda left some money for me in the game," Smoky complained. He vanished from sight. Slocum took the opportunity to move another fifteen yards upslope.

From his new vantage point he saw the two men standing close by in a hollow. One held out a tobacco pouch for the other. In less than a minute tiny plumes of smoke rose from two cigarettes. Slocum shook his head at such carelessness. Even if he hadn't seen the man against the sky, he couldn't have missed the sight of the smoke columns or the heavy tobacco odor on the wind.

They were only miners, he told himself, not trained soldiers. From the way they carried their rifles, they knew little about marksmanship. One slammed his carbine down against a rock so hard, it must have moved the back sights. The other let his rifle fall over, getting dirt in the barrel. When he noticed, he just tapped it out rather than looking to clean it right away.

If Slocum showed himself to the men, they'd be lucky if their weapons didn't explode in their hands. But Slocum was careful. He waited until Smoky picked up his rifle and wandered back down the ravine leading toward the stone fortress.

From this angle Slocum got a better look at it, nestled between the two hills. The road he had taken petered out and turned into the ravine. Why the road had been cut in the barren landscape was beyond him, but he was glad that it had. Trying to get a wagon filled with explosives across the rocky terrain would have been too dangerous.

As it stood, the only danger was to Henry Hackett and the men with him.

The new sentry finished his smoke, then found a shady spot and sat down. He tipped his hat forward, and in a few minutes Slocum heard loud snoring. Slocum knew it wasn't a trick. Nothing either of the lookouts had done showed any competence. An entire army could have ridden up the ravine to the rear of the fortress.

Slocum picked his way through the stony ground until he came to the sleeping sentry. Something caused the man to stir. Slocum measured his target, then swung the butt of his rifle. It crunched firmly against the man's head. He slumped over, knocked out. Slocum spent a few minutes tying the man's hands and feet. For good measure he used the man's own bandanna to gag him.

"Sleep tight," Slocum said. "You may not know it, but you're one of the lucky ones in this pig shoot."

Slocum had no real quarrel with this nameless miner. He wanted Hackett. Only if he had to kill to get to the fat mine owner would he take a life.

He was saving all his hate for the leader, not the paid followers.

It took the better part of three hours for him to position the dynamite along the ravine where it would do the most good. Finished, he climbed back to the sentry post. He had no idea how long each stint was.

The guard had regained consciousness and glowered at Slocum. Slocum was too busy studying the heavily fortified house and the steep hills on either side to pay much attention. Using Stevenson's telescope, he focused on the stone walls.

"Too high to climb," he said, more to himself than to the guard. "Just about as I figured."

He turned the scope to the hillsides and found two or three likely places where he could position himself with the three cases of dynamite he hadn't planted along the ravine. A direct assault on the thick stone walls was suicidal.

Dropping dynamite into the enclosure wasn't too promising, either. The distance might be too great to toss a lit stick. But the rocky ledges and overhangs on the hillside gave Slocum the idea of starting avalanches. If that didn't unnerve the miners guarding Hackett, he didn't know what would. Even though they weren't underground, the noise and sight of so much falling rock would send them scuttling out like dung beetles to a cow pie.

The sentry kicked and tried to get free. Slocum shook his head. The man wasn't too bright. Slocum was obviously leaving. He ought to have saved his struggles until after his captor had left.

Slocum walked over to the man, judged the distance again, and swung. The rifle butt slammed hard into the man's skull. His head snapped back, and once more he was out like a light.

By the time he woke up and Slocum had returned, Hackett's sanctuary would be turned into a living hell.

17

Slocum felt added pressure on him to finish this distasteful chore. The hot spring sun would be setting within two hours. He had to be back around the hill and in position by then. Otherwise his small kindness in letting the careless sentry live would come back to haunt him. Hackett would find the dynamite planted throughout the ravine and figure out what Slocum planned.

The murderous mine owner might just turn tail and run, forcing Slocum to hunt him down like a dog. It was better if Slocum kept them all bottled up and, only when he was ready, let them come rushing out to the slaughter. Most of those holed up with Hackett were innocent men, hard-rock miners in his pay who had no stake in their boss' back-stabbing scheme.

He unhitched the team, leaving the heavy wagon hidden the best he could, around a curve in the road. Alternating between the horses, he rode hell-bent for leather to return to the rise where he had left Carter Stevenson earlier in the day. To his disgust the man hadn't gone back to Leadville, as Slocum had wanted.

Stevenson waved jovially when he spotted Slocum.

"I say, this is getting good. There's some sort of activity in the fort," Stevenson said. He had a twin to the telescope Slocum had left behind overlooking the ravine.

"You're not going to like what's going to happen," Slocum said. "I wanted you to go to the club and forget this. There's no need to come back until the dust settles."

"Ah, but, Mr. Slocum, there is. You forget Henry tried to *kill* me. It was only through your kind intervention that prevented my death. He ought to be brought to justice. I want to be here when he is."

Slocum stared sharply at the mine owner. Something in his tone didn't jibe with his happy-go-lucky words. A core of steel hid inside Stevenson. Slocum wasn't sure he had ever penetrated the man's clever façade. As if aware of Slocum's scrutiny, Stevenson reached into his inner coat pocket and pulled out a flask. He took enough of a draft to choke a mule.

He silently proffered the flask to Slocum. On impulse, Slocum took it. The sharp sting of brandy burned his tongue and mouth as he sampled some of the potion.

"Good, eh, Mr. Slocum? Another drink?"

Slocum shook his head and handed back the silver flask. "Don't need more. I want a clear head for this rabbit shoot."

"You have them bottled up?" Stevenson's voice carried an eagerness Slocum had heard only in men used to murdering in cold blood.

"Reckon so." Slocum checked the Winchester and levered a round into its oily chamber. He fumbled through a pile of supplies he'd brought and found several boxes of ammunition. He thrust these into his coat pockets. His spare Navy Colt slid into his belt, as did enough ammo for both side arms. He was going up against an army; he had to be prepared to fight like one himself.

"Will you allow me to aid you?"

Slocum didn't think he could do this alone. But he had no choice.

"You're not much good with a six-shooter, are you?"

"Well . . ." Stevenson's voice trailed off. This was as good an answer as any he could have given, surrounded as he was by his six-bit words and fancy-ass way of speaking.

"I'll deal with Hackett."

"I can get any number of men to help on the expedition. There are men from my own mine who wouldn't be averse to earning a few extra dollars for such work."

"This isn't their fight. I'm a mite disgusted at the way Hackett got his own people to guard him."

"He isn't much of a man, is he?"

Slocum didn't answer. He didn't think too highly of Carter Stevenson, either. The man drank heavily, wasted his money on bad bets at the racetrack, played poker with reckless abandon, and seemed to have no redeeming virtues other than being filthy rich from the sweat and blood of others. Even exalted wealth wasn't enough to do him any real good, Slocum decided.

There was a reason shrouds didn't have pockets. Nobody took their money with them. Not Carter Stevenson. Not even Henry Hackett.

"I've got to get back," Slocum said.

"Up there on the rise? Overlooking Hackett's fortress?" Stevenson pulled out the topographic map and spread it on the ground. Wind whipped down off the mountains. He pinned each corner with a heavy rock, then bent forward, studying the map carefully.

Slocum had no more time to waste. The sun would be going down too soon, and he had to root the bastards out of their hidey-hole by then or he'd lose them in the dark.

"Wait, Mr. Slocum. Here . . . is this where you're going to position yourself?"

Slocum compared the map with the spot he had scouted.

From the ridge to the south of Hackett's stronghold rose a short spire that was just about perfect for him. A good marksman could command both the front and back of the fortress.

And Slocum was the best.

"Just about there," Slocum said. "What difference does it make?"

"None. I just want to be sure of my facts. 'Never leap before you look,' that's what my father always told me."

" 'Never look back' is better advice," Slocum said.

Stevenson laughed unexpectedly. "That is rich, Mr. Slocum. Never look back because something may be catching up with you. That's *very* good."

"Glad you like it."

"Is there anything you need? Anything at all?"

Slocum paused, then smiled crookedly. "One of those fancy cigars you smoke would be nice."

"Of course, sir. It is my pleasure." Stevenson opened a gold-inlaid case holding five plump, rich cigars and held it out for Slocum. His nose twitched at the odor rising from the case. Slocum took the nearest one. It wasn't for pleasure that he wanted the cigar. He thrust it into his pocket where it wouldn't get broken.

Slocum swung back onto one of the team. The other he had packed with the three cases of extra dynamite. He had some distance to go, and he might have to fight his way through another of Hackett's sentries. From the way the fat mine owner ordered his troops it wasn't likely, but Slocum wasn't taking any chance of being held up. The slowly setting sun was his worst enemy at the moment.

He heard Stevenson behind him, cackling like a hen sitting on a nest full of eggs. Slocum decided he would be well rid of the man soon enough.

And of Henry Hackett. His hands clenched into tight fists as he thought of the dead Linette. It had been on Hackett's order that Griff had shotgunned her. Hackett would pay, just as his foreman had. Just as Harrison and the third man who had shot up Angelica Clayton's wedding. They'd all paid with their lives.

Hackett was left.

Slocum got to the base of the ridge and started up. It took almost an hour for him to wind his way back and forth along the barren face of the hill. The complaining horses were tuckered out and unable to continue by the time he reached his aerie. He jumped to the ground. His mount let out a long, wet whinny of relief. The other horse bearing the crates of explosive was less tired but still happy to stop the insane climb up the steep hill.

Slocum scouted the area to be sure he wasn't going to be seen by any of Hackett's guards. He shook his head. The nearest sentry post was three quarters of the way down the hill toward the fortress. That guard would die quickly once Slocum got to work. He would be able to get much closer than he'd thought. He would be able to throw dynamite straight into the compound and not blow half the damn mountain apart in order to chase Hackett from his hidey-hole.

The only other post appeared to be the one Slocum had already found along the back ravine. Hackett might be scared, but he wasn't scared enough to post lookouts in the right places.

Squinting into the sun, Slocum estimated he had an hour before twilight robbed him of good light for his massacre. He squatted down and worked on the packages of dynamite he was going to deliver. Three sticks went into each bundle, along with a blasting cap and eighteen inches of black fuse.

Twenty minutes later Slocum was ready. He unloaded his pockets and put the boxes of rifle cartridges where he could get at them. He settled down, moved a few rocks to afford him a comfortable resting spot, then pulled out the cigar he had taken from Stevenson. He flicked a lucifer and coaxed it into a steady flame, then applied it to the cut end of the cigar. Deep puffs brought a bright coal to the tip.

He wished he had time to enjoy the smoke. He didn't. This was necessary for the attack. Slocum shifted the cigar to the corner of his mouth and lit the fuse sticking out of a dynamite bundle. The fuse sizzled and hissed and popped. When it had burned down three quarters of the way, Slocum reared back and heaved.

His aim was deadly. The explosive landed just above the sentry. The man turned curiously, his head bobbing as if it had been put on a spring. He never knew what happened. The dynamite exploded and sent a grisly shower down over Hackett's fortress.

Before the first dynamite had gone off, Slocum was lighting the fuses on half a dozen other bundles. His arm grew stiff from the mighty heaves it took to lob the dynamite inside Hackett's stone-walled stronghold.

The first of the bundles didn't go off. Slocum didn't worry about it. The black fuse was reliable; the blasting caps weren't. The next five bundles all exploded, one blowing open the heavy-timbered gate leading into the fortress.

Hell broke loose then. Slocum heard Hackett's shrill screams, demanding that his men protect him. The dust and debris settled slowly. The dynamite that had opened the heavy gates completely disorganized any defense. The miners thought an army was rushing in on them. No one noticed the explosion had come from inside, not out.

Slocum puffed a few more times on the cigar to keep it going, then picked up the rifle. Settling down as comfortably as he could, he started to work. The first bullet missed a miner running in panic from the front gate. The second slug caught the fleeing man in the leg and sent him cartwheeling down the rocky road.

Ignoring him, not wanting to kill for the sake of killing,

Slocum turned his attention back to the seething cauldron within the fort. A few well-placed shots was all it took to start the men firing at each other. They had no idea where the attack came from. Lacking a real leader, they succumbed quickly to fear.

Slocum squinted to get a better look at the men in the fortress. None mattered save Henry Hackett. Of the fat mining magnate he saw nothing. Slocum didn't think Hackett had escaped.

He hefted his Winchester and began firing again with a measured cadence, each shot seeking flesh. Most of his carefully aimed shots missed. It hardly mattered, owing to the panic they caused. Slocum wasn't out for murder; he wanted confusion in the ranks of his enemy.

He succeeded. It looked more like an anthill with boiling water poured down it than any military installation.

Above the sound of the gunfire came a bellow. Someone sought to regain control. The miners were their own worst enemies, and Slocum wanted to keep it that way. He sighted in on the miner, trying to restore order. He emptied the Winchester, then reloaded and emptied its magazine again before he drove the miner back to cover.

Slocum puffed a few times on the half-ash cigar and lit a few more bundles of dynamite. Heaving them as hard as he could, he reached the far side of Hackett's fort. Two of the explosive packages blew out a portion of the wall. This renewed the fear inside the fortress that they were under assault from an army.

A few well-placed bullets convinced eight men to burst from the sundered front gate and run for their lives. Slocum figured they might stop running at about the time they got to Leadville. Or maybe they'd just keep on going, thinking everyone was out to get them.

He sprayed more bullets into the fortress until the hammer fell on an empty chamber. He reloaded and waited a few minutes before continuing. The barrel of the Winchester was getting hot. Slocum had been in gunfights before in which he had melted the barrel. To do that now was to let Hackett escape.

"Up the hill!" came the cry. "The attack's coming from above the sentry post!"

Slocum had wondered how long it would take before someone pinpointed the source of their misery. Bullets began ricocheting off the rocks around him. He huddled down and let the leaden rain sail on by. The horses were safely beyond the curve of the hill, and Slocum was partially protected by the boulders between himself and the fort.

"We got him. He ain't firing no more" came the optimistic cry. Two others tried to talk sense into the man making the wild assumption that Slocum was dead. It did no good. The miner rushed out and began scrambling up the slope to see the result of his marksmanship.

Slocum let him get almost all the way up before rising, sighting, and squeezing the trigger. The man's arms flapped wildly, as if he wanted to take flight. He tumbled backward down the hill, half rolling, half sliding. Slocum followed the body with two more bundles of dynamite. The cascade of rock, dust, and pieces of corpse dashed whatever courage remained in the fort's defenders.

"You can't go. Don't leave. I'm paying you, dammit!"

Slocum recognized Henry Hackett's pleas. He rose up and looked around for the fat man. At first he didn't see him in the rush to get out of the fort. The miners realized they were being shot down like rats. Slocum wondered if it was the fire from the Winchester that had driven them out or if it was the dynamite. Few, if any, had ever faced a man with a gun in his hand. They all lived with the knowledge of the deadly power of dynamite.

Hackett came through the smoke and dust like a juggernaut. Slocum had to give the mine owner credit for some courage. He held a six-shooter in each pudgy hand. The determination in his stride belied the fright in his voice, demanding that the miners stay to protect him.

Slocum sighted in and squeezed off a shot. He cursed as he missed. At this range his target had to remain still for several seconds or keep walking in a straight line at a steady pace. Hackett was jerking around, snapping out orders and changing direction constantly.

A few more shots convinced Slocum he wasn't going to hit Hackett with the Winchester. He wished he had a big rifle, a Sharps .69 or some other rifle with a tripod. Not only would the heavy slug cut through just about anything and kill anyone it hit, the rifles were damn accurate.

"Get out, you damn fool!" roared one miner. He tried to shake some sense into Henry Hackett. The mine owner turned and fired point-blank. The miner fell like a marionette with its strings cut.

Slocum held back from firing again. His Winchester was loaded and he needed every shot. He had a feeling in his bones about what was going to happen next. To hasten the end, he knocked the ash off the inch of cigar remaining and lit the fuses on the last of his dynamite. He started tossing the dynamite. His arm was giving out. Only one packet reached the stone fort. It blew out a huge hunk of wall but did no significant damage.

Through the blasted hell below, Slocum saw a man mounting a horse. It had to be Henry Hackett getting ready to flee.

Slocum smiled when he saw Hackett turn his steed toward the rear of the fort. He hadn't seen any way out—but one had been there. Hackett put his heels to his horse's flanks once he got away from his stone fortress.

Slocum rested the Winchester in a rocky vee and squeezed off a round. It missed its target by inches. Hackett hunkered down over his horse's neck, but he wasn't Slocum's target.

The next shot found a case of dynamite buried halfway up the side of the ravine.

A landslide forced Hackett to veer sharply and go up out of the ravine, taking a slower path along the rocky terrain.

Slocum kept shooting—and the hidden cases of dynamite kept erupting. Huge gouts of flame and rock blasted into the twilight, blocking the path of the fleeing Henry Hackett.

Slocum's Winchester came up empty. He cursed as he reloaded. He hadn't slowed Hackett enough. Reloading, he returned the rifle to its vee and started firing faster.

Three more cases of dynamite detonated. This was enough to bring down a rocky ledge and the hundreds of tons of debris above it. As if flowing through molasses, the boulders began slipping down the side of the steep hill. It gained speed as the rock gathered up loose stone along the way. By the time it reached the ravine, it had swept with it everything living in its path.

Slocum stood. In the dusk he made out the mine owner's dead horse. Of the horse's rider he saw no trace.

Slocum reloaded his Winchester as he went back to his team of horses. Henry Hackett wouldn't elude him this time. He'd see the man's dead body or know the reason.

18

The draft horse wasn't up to the trip back down the hillside in the gathering gloom. Slocum wished he had the gelding he'd left back at his base camp. He considered making a detour and getting it, then decided against it. Henry Hackett wasn't going far—but Slocum didn't want to lose him in the dark. Without any daylight to guide him, the road around the mountain was too long for Slocum to retrace easily.

At the base of the hill he turned the protesting horse's head directly toward the burned-out stone fort. Flames still licked hungrily at some of the inner structures, and holes gaped in the walls where his dynamite had blown out huge chunks of stone and mortar. He passed several of the miners who had been entrusted with protecting Henry Hackett. They paid him no nevermind. They were too intent on hauling ass back to Leadville.

Slocum let them be. His quarrel wasn't with them. He wanted their boss.

He got to the front of the fort. A few men cried out in pain, trapped inside the burning structure. Slocum ignored their pleas for aid. There was no need to gun down the men.

181

He saw no reason to rescue them, either. He made his way through the debris and found the back door Hackett had used, thinking to sneak down the ravine. Following this path saved Slocum more than an hour of travel in the twilight.

On the path, he quickly found the result of his dynamiting. Huge boulders forced him away from the route, out of the ravine and to higher ground where the going got tricky. Slocum had to dismount and lead his horse when the fragmented rock underfoot got too treacherous.

His progress was slowed even more a half mile from the fort when he came to the avalanche area. He had brought down better than half the mountain on Hackett's head. But he had seen the bloated mine owner after the rockfall. His horse might be buried up to its hindquarters, but Hackett was still free somewhere.

Slocum discovered the horse's remains a few minutes later. Rocks had lacerated it beyond any hope of salvation. From the way it had thrashed about, it had died in considerable pain. Hackett hadn't been man enough to put the animal out of its misery.

Slocum wouldn't make the same mistake with Hackett.

A bullet whined off a nearby rock. Slocum dived for cover. A second bullet brought his horse down to its knees. Slocum saw pink froth boiling from the injured animal's nostrils and knew the slug had pierced a lung. Coldness welling inside, Slocum turned his Winchester toward the horse and squeezed off a shot. The horse let out a single neigh, collapsed to its knees, then fell heavily, not moving.

He turned his attention back to the source of the gunfire. When a foot-long tongue of flame reached into the night, Slocum pinpointed his target. He sighted carefully and pulled off a shot. Loud cursing was followed by deathly silence. Slocum wasn't gulled into believing he had killed

Hackett. At best he had driven the man farther down the ravine. With both of them on foot, the hunt was one-sided.

Hackett was fat and no match for Slocum and his wrath.

Slocum slipped to his left, going uphill, trying to gain the high ground over Hackett. When he got to a spot he thought was adequate for an ambush, he cautiously peered down toward the debris-filled ravine. He didn't see the mine owner anywhere.

Straining, Slocum listened for the sound of the fat man's lungs heaving in the high altitude. He heard soft, muffled sounds but couldn't identify them. He decided he didn't have to. They weren't made by any nocturnal animal; that left only Henry Hackett.

Making his way as soft as a shadow crossing another shadow, Slocum stalked Hackett. Movement a dozen yards ahead of him caused Slocum to hike his rifle to his shoulder, sight, and fire.

A loud screech of pain was his reward. He hadn't killed Hackett but had seriously wounded him.

"Who is it?" demanded Hackett. "Don't kill me. I'm not armed."

"You've got a brace of six-shooters," Slocum said, contradicting him. "I saw them."

"All right, I lied. I . . . I'm scared. Don't kill me and I'll pay you good. What do you want? I'm rich. Take it all! Just don't kill me!"

"I want your hide, that's what I want," Slocum said. He ducked down when Hackett began firing wildly into the dark. Slocum didn't want to stay in one place too long. Hackett would likely get lucky with his undisciplined shooting if he did.

Slocum heard more scurrying sounds. He frowned. Those weren't noises made by a critically wounded man. He approached more carefully, thinking he might have missed

Hackett altogether and that the man was laying a trap for him.

He came to the spot where Hackett had been. The puddle of blood on the rock being sucked into the thirsty ground left no doubt that Hackett had been hit.

Slocum looked around but heard and saw nothing. Dropping flat onto his belly, he began sniffing for the coppery scent of spilled blood. His nose gave him the trail when his eyes failed at the task. The droplets led downhill. Only after a few yards did he see the twin ruts being cut into the ground.

He stared at them and thought hard.

"I'm coming for you, Hackett. I know you're wounded real bad."

He lifted his hat on the end of his rifle barrel. A half dozen shots cut the hat to ribbons and knocked the rifle from his hand. Slocum scuttled along on his belly and retrieved the Winchester, then discarded it. A slug had ripped through the side and jammed the receiver. It'd take a skilled gunsmith a week of Sundays to fix it.

"You there, Slocum? Or did I do for you?"

The voice was muffled and low. Slocum didn't respond. He began moving to his left, circling before he approached the source of the fusillade. It took a spell. By the time he got to a boulder looking down on a niche in the rock, he had wasted well nigh ten minutes.

He peered down at Henry Hackett. There was no mistaking the man's flopping jowls. He lay on his back, his hand clutching his side. Blood oozed slowly through the layers of clothing and onto the ground. Slocum had sorely wounded him. Near his hand rested a six-shooter.

"No," Hackett moaned. Slocum drew the Navy Colt thrust into his belt and brought it to bear, thinking Hackett had seen him. He hesitated when a shadow below him moved.

"Yes, dear Henry, I am afraid this is the way it has to

be. You've told me all I need to know." Carter Stevenson leveled his pistol and squeezed off a round. Henry Hackett's corpulent body tensed as the bullet ripped through his chest, then he sagged in death.

Slocum went cold to the center of his being. Stevenson had shown no remorse in killing his rival. He had simply walked up and killed him. Or had he just arrived?

In his surprise Slocum got careless. A pebble rolled under his boot. Stevenson spun and fired. The slug whined off into the night, missing Slocum by several feet. Slocum's reaction, though, was wrong. He jerked hard to one side and lost his balance.

He tumbled to the sandy pit below, his Colt spinning from his hand.

"Mr. Slocum, you are far more resourceful than I'd have thought." Stevenson edged around. "Don't," the foppish mine owner warned, the six-shooter in his hand unwavering.

"You tried to kill me a while back," Slocum accused. "I thought it was Hackett, but it was you who shot up my hat."

"I fell for that old trick. My, my, I am slipping. I didn't want to leave poor Henry to check my marksmanship, though. That was obviously a mistake. I shan't repeat it. Everything else has worked out so wondrously well."

Slocum came to a sitting position, keeping his jacket pulled over his cross-draw holster and the other Navy Colt resting there.

"Why did you wait so long to kill Hackett?"

"You saw that, eh?" Stevenson shook his head. "A pity. I must kill you also, not that I wouldn't have, anyway. You are a loose end, and I hate loose ends."

"But Hackett—"

"The fool." Steel came into Stevenson's normally soft voice. "He tried to double-cross me. He sent Harrison and Griff to kill me!"

"I saved you from them," Slocum said, realizing he hadn't done anyone any favors with the act.

"That's the only reason you're still alive. But you should savor each fleeting second. There won't be many left to you."

"You and Hackett were involved in a plot?" Slocum asked. Everything began falling into place for him. "You and Hackett were driving out the other mine owners and buying up their claims."

"Of course we were. I used poor Henry as my front. Who would ever think silly old Carter Stevenson could do a thing like kill another human being? If anything had gone wrong, Henry would have been blamed and I would have taken it all. As it stands, he has been removed . . . by a drifter named John Slocum."

Slocum fought to keep from reaching for his pistol. He needed an edge and he didn't see it yet. Stevenson would grow careless. Then Slocum would act.

"Why?"

"Why? I am surprised at your lack of imagination, Mr. Slocum. Millions of dollars in silver flow through Leadville every year. But it is split hundreds—thousands!—of ways. How inefficient. It is far better if it all came to rest in just one pocket."

"Yours?"

"Yes, of course. Hackett was supposed to deal with the other officers of the Iron-Silver Mining Company. His methods were so crude and inept. That you are here is testimony to that."

"What about the wedding? Was that all Hackett's doing?"

"Oh, yes. But Griff's attack on you was all my doing. He worked for whoever paid him the most. I convinced him that he could save his putrid life if he did as I told him.

Thank you for killing him. I would have had to deal with him myself."

"You ordered him to kill me—and he killed Linette instead."

"Alas, Griff was not the finest instrument to use for such a demanding task. Of course he killed your whore."

Slocum went cold inside. He rolled forward and came to his knees. His coat fell free. He could reach his six-shooter if he wanted.

"That's it?" asked Slocum. "All this killing was the result of greed and double crossing?"

"What else is there, Mr. Slocum?" Stevenson's hand moved slightly, showing he was preparing to fire.

Slocum's hand flashed like lightning to his pistol. Stevenson squeezed off the first shot; it went wide of its target.

Slocum's slug ripped out Stevenson's heart.

He cocked the single-action pistol for another shot. It wasn't needed. Carter Stevenson was dead. Slocum got to his feet and went to the mine owner's side. Papers thrust into his pocket began to soak up blood. Slocum plucked them from the pocket and peered at them in the darkness.

The names scrawled on the bottom of the last page were those of Henry Hackett and Carter Stevenson. The papers proved their illicit alliance to squeeze out or kill other mine owners in Leadville. Slocum had no need for them. He stuffed the documents back into Stevenson's pocket. The man had probably taken them off Hackett and hadn't had the time to destroy them.

A horse whinnied. Slocum turned his back on the two dead men and found his gelding. Stevenson had ridden around the mountain on the gelding, thinking to leave it and further incriminate Slocum the instant Slocum had left to begin his assault on Hackett's fortress. All Stevenson had to do was wait for Hackett to be flushed out like quail.

Slocum had done it for him. And Slocum had ended Stevenson's loathsome life to boot.

He mounted the horse and turned its head for Wyoming Territory. He didn't want to return to Leadville. There would be hell to pay when it was learned that two of the most powerful men in town had been killed. More than this, for Slocum, Leadville held too many painful memories, of Linette, of the better times she had brought, of the promise for the future she had given him.